Dot to Dot

...

Kit Bakke

Also by Kit Bakke

Miss Alcott's E-Mail

Hotel Angeline: A Novel in 36 Voices, (Chapter 21)

*Hilda Evangeline Silva Sprague:
A Century (and Counting) in the Pacific Northwest*

Copyright ©2011 Kit Bakke
All Rights Reserved

ISBN: 1456368044
ISBN-13: 9781456368043

To all the nieces and daughters in the world,
And the aunts and mothers who love them.

• • •

"Neither Absence nor Distance
nor Time can ever break the Chain."

Dorothy Wordsworth, 1788

• • •

"Tell Mr. Cyrus I'm running into a lot of history here, and it's even messier than he thinks."

Dot to Junie, 2011

Praise for Miss Alcott's E-Mail

"Alcott fans will enjoy the biographical essays and keen manner in which Bakke assumes Alcott's voice and connects two distant eras. Readers interested in the 1960s protest movement will also find much to consider in Bakke's frank assessments of her own turbulent young adulthood."

— *Booklist*

• • •

"Brimming with meticulous research and unusual insights, Miss Alcott's E-Mail brings Louisa May Alcott back into our midst, in all her light and dark complexity. Kit Bakke's fresh new look at Louisa May reminds us that this spirited and brave reformer was by no means a little woman."

— Geraldine Brooks, bestselling author of *March*

• • •

"The effect is like a wonderful movie shot with a hand-held camera."

— Carolyn See in *The Washington Post*

• • •

This work is a delight. Recommended for all libraries.

— *Library Journal*

Praise for Dot to Dot

"*Dot to Dot* is a wonderful and endearing story about the power of books and travel to heal us. Kit Bakke has written a young adult novel that is a perfect mother-daughter book. Following Dot's trip to England with her eccentric aunt takes the reader on a touching and fantastical journey that also cleverly celebrates the wisdom of Jane Austen and other inspiring women writers of her era."

Jim Lynch, author of national bestseller *The Highest Tide*

• • •

"*Dot to Dot* is a tale of a plucky young teen's journey through grief after her mother's horrific death. Reluctantly, Dot embarks on a trip to England with an oddball aunt who is now her guardian. Once in the old-world land of Jane Austen, Mary Shelly and other inspiring females, however, Dot is enchanted to discover rather magical and amazing things about herself, her mother and modern life."

Jennie Shortridge, best-selling author of *When She Flew*

Dorothy Mary-Jane's
ENGLAND

Contents

Part I: Death 1

The Red Tsunami. 3
Aunt Tab Appears 7
BT/AT. 11
A Failed Try. 17
Packing What Matters. 21

Part II: Destinations & Detours 25

A Terrible Start 27
Soup's On. 33
Eavesdropping on Enlightenment. 39
Sad and Mad. 45
Connecting the Dots. 53
Frankenstein's Mother 59
A Good Laugh 63
Lost 71
Smoke Signals 81
Miss Austen's Room. 85
Sugar Bowl. 91
Good Stuff, Bad Stuff. 97
Somebody Has to Push. 101

Part III: Decisions ...107

Nick-spotting... 109
The Star of Alethea... 113
Less Drama Is Better... 119
Aunt Tab Spouts Poetry... 125
Two Months Ago Today... 129
Feeling Safe... 133
Open Heart, Open Mind... 137
Dot to the Rescue... 143
Nick, Again... 147
Dear Mom... 157
The Tarot Speaks... 163
Wishes to Ashes... 173
Third and Last... 175
Time to Decide... 181

MORE, if you are interested... 187

Part I: Death

One: The Red Tsunami

Dot's lengthening twelve-year-old body lay curled on her ratty Tinkerbell rug. She should have given Tink away years ago, along with her thrift-store Lego people and her Frog and Toad books. But she didn't, and now she knew she never could. They were the only real family she had left.

Dot tried to curve herself into the exact shape of the short-haired pixie stitched into the shaggy round rug. She kept her eyes wide open, anchored to the yellow wall opposite her unmade bed. Dot and her mother had painted her room last summer, picking out a sunny color that matched the insides of the Shasta daisies that bloomed in huge, floppy clumps in their narrow backyard. Although the cheerful color didn't really help, it wasn't as bad as it might have been.

"Damn glad we didn't pick red," Dot whispered to the yellow wall, knowing her mother wouldn't have minded the swearing one bit.

The main difference between Dot and Tinkerbell on the rug was that the pixie's right arm was stretched high over her head, pointing her magic wand and spewing silvery threads across the rug's dark blue background. Dot, though, pressed her arms tightly against her body, taking up as little space as possible. Whether she was holding herself in or fighting the world off, she couldn't say.

Thea, her mother, would have known which (likely it was both), and right away she would have said the precisely perfect words to open Dot back up. But Thea wasn't around anymore.

Thea had died a week ago and now the funeral was over. Only Dot and her Aunt Tab, and Thea, sort of, had been there, so it wasn't much

One: The Red Tsunami

of a ceremony. Dot had mostly kept her eyes closed, which wasn't a good strategy. Open was better because it helped to block the bad memories. But open was bad too, because whatever she looked at reminded her of how empty and useless and stupid the world had become.

"We'll take the ashes home so we can figure out what Thea would like done with them," Aunt Tab had said, which Dot thought was creepy, and she'd said so, too, in a loud voice. Not that Aunt Tab had paid any attention. Aunt Tab was just another part of the barren world that no longer made sense and obviously didn't care.

"I'm just a dot of nothing," Dot whispered to Tink. She didn't expect Tinkerbell to answer back, and even if she could, Dot didn't expect her to make things right. Nothing was ever going to be right again, not ever.

Not since Dot had seen her mother's blood all over the sidewalk. When she shut her eyes, an ugly tsunami of memories poured into her brain, filling every crevice with devastation. Red, such a bad red. Nothing good could ever come from such a terrible red. Dot stared at her yellow wall, her gaze raking across Tinkerbell's big eyes and perky nose and out over the rug's tufted blue background. There were flecks of dust and silvery threads in the blue tufts, but no red at all. The blue yarn and the yellow walls were absolutely not red. Dot hung on to that fuzzy blue and the bright yellow with little safety pins that streamed out of her mind, hooking her to any image that wasn't her mother's body spread out in that odd posture, partly on the sidewalk and partly on the street, and the evil red puddle spreading all around her.

No one had expected Dot's mother to die. It was a freak accident, Dot heard the medic say when he screeched the van into the Emergency Room driveway of the hospital and doctors and nurses ran out to rush Thea's prone body through a door labeled Major Procedures. Although everyone moved quickly, it was already too late to do anything but talk.

Staring at the blue yarn or the yellow walls wasn't enough to block the pictures of that cloudy Saturday afternoon. Dot couldn't stop them from unreeling over and over again in her mind. Against her will, she watched her mother and herself leave their neighborhood branch of the

Seattle Public Library, as they'd done hundreds of times ever since Dot was two years old, happily loaded with two weeks' worth of adventure, fun and, just possibly, wisdom.

Next she saw her mother and herself outside the library entrance, holding their books and pointing at the clouds in the sky with their free hands. Dot remembered every word of their discussion about the definite preponderance of nimbostratus formations. They agreed it might rain soon, so they decided they'd better take the bus instead of walking. Most of Dot and Thea's decisions were like that—choices made together after an interesting chat. Thea always said she learned as much as Dot when they talked like that, which always made Dot feel good.

Dot stared harder at the tufts of blue, trying like crazy to hang on and not go past the cloud conversation. But she failed, like she always had this past week, and the next memory reel started up, the one where she walked to the corner with her mother. For the millionth time Dot watched as she and her mother stood waiting for the light to change so they could cross over to their bus stop. Then came the completely and totally unstoppable scene—the part when the big red trailer truck roared by and its huge, sticking-out side-view mirror hit Thea right at eye level. Dot heard the damp thudding sound echo again and again as it smashed the top of her mother's head and broke her neck. It was over in a flash.

Dot never imagined the world could change so fast. One second she had a mother, and the next second she didn't. One second she was an ordinary kid with ordinary problems, a second later she was an orphan who was afraid of everything. It wasn't just her mother who had lost her hold on life.

Two: Aunt Tab Appears

Dot had stood there on the sidewalk, eyes wildly looking in every direction, her whole body tensed, begging, pleading time to go backward, just for that one second, that's all she needed. It wouldn't take much to push her mother back a step or two on the sidewalk, toward the library entrance. Just a little nudge and everything would go back to normal. Please, please.

But nothing changed. There was Thea—it was impossible not to notice that she wasn't herself anymore, her legs at strange angles on the sidewalk and the rest of her draped awkwardly over the curb into the street. Library books, now wet and red, were scattered all around her messed-up head.

A medic van arrived quickly and men and women who appeared to know what they were doing kneeled in the red puddle, huddling over broken-up Thea. They carefully laid her on a stretcher and bundled her into the back of their van. Dot could see a shadowy red halo seep onto the white cloth at one end of the stretcher.

"That's my mother," Dot managed to say as they were closing the door.

"Come with us, then. You can ride in front."

It didn't take long to reach the hospital. The medic van backed into the Emergency entrance and Dot watched the doctors and nurses rush Thea into the Major Procedures Room. Through the open door, Dot could see bright lights and walls lined with shelves and tubes and shiny electrical machinery. Then a nurse parked Dot in a blue plastic chair in the hall and

Two: Aunt Tab Appears

closed the door to the Major Procedures Room. Dot sat completely still, never moving her eyes from the door that separated her from her mother.

It was as if time had stopped, but in the completely wrong place. Perhaps if she kept extremely still, the past, the right past, the one when her mother was okay, would fly back in, like last summer when that iridescent hummingbird had landed on her knee as she was sitting very quietly, reading by the trumpet vine patch in her backyard.

After about a half hour of not moving, Dot watched the Major Procedures door open. A nurse pushed a different cart with high canvas sides out of the room and wheeled it down the hall, away from the Emergency entrance. She disappeared behind a set of double doors that automatically opened and closed with a quiet swish.

Then another nurse with a kind and sad face came over to Dot and put her arms around her shoulders.

"Let's go sit in here," she said and led the way to a little room nearby. The label on its door said Quiet Room. Inside were a couch, a cushioned chair, a coffee table, and a phone. There was a poster on one wall of a rose garden in full bloom with a fountain in the middle. The roses were red.

"We need to call your father and tell him about your mother."

"I don't have a father."

"Is there a grandmother, or an aunt, maybe?"

"I guess. Maybe Aunt Tab." Dot couldn't tell if she was whispering or shouting or just thinking the words. She was trying to avoid the red roses, which were jostling and crowding her in a scary way. The world was as wobbly and crooked as a Halloween haunted house, and there was a lot of feedback screeching in her ears.

The nurse must have figured it out, though, and when Aunt Tab came stalking into the Quiet Room it got unquiet really quick.

"What's going on around here? Where's Thea? Where's the doctor? Dorothy Mary-Jane!" she shouted as she galumphed over to Dot like a flapping flamingo and enfolded her in an awkward and bony hug. Dot didn't respond, but she didn't resist either. What was the point? There was no point to anything anymore.

• • •

Aunt Tab lived by herself on the other side of Seattle from Dot, but the day Thea died, she began staying at Dot's house. "Until we get things sorted out," Aunt Tab had said, her searchlight eyes piercing through Dot's brain. Dot didn't think Aunt Tab was asking permission, so she didn't say anything.

Aunt Tab was pretty much a stranger, and a strange stranger at that. She was one of those abrupt people who suddenly materialize, act like they run the show, and then disappear. Hard to get to know. Thea had once told Dot that Tab had the Big Sister Gene in spades. Bossy, very bossy.

Dot used to imagine what it would be like to have a big sister. Or to be a big sister; either seemed great to her. They'd be best friends and hang out all the time, even when they were teenagers and grown-ups. Her next door neighbor Junie was about as close as she'd gotten to a sister. Junie was her best friend. Except for her mother, of course.

All roads led back to Thea.

There was no way not to think about her.

But Thea and her sister Tab seemed to hang out not at all. Aunt Tab came over for Christmas and for Dot's birthday, and since those happened on the exact same day, it meant Dot and her Aunt Tab had never spent much time together. The sisters didn't act as if they'd had a fight or were angry with each other; they just didn't seem to get much out of each other's company. "Sisters don't automatically have a lot in common," Thea had once said to Dot. "You'll see how different Jane Austen made the sisters in her books. Next year we'll read *Pride and Prejudice*."

But at least Dot and Aunt Tab had recognized each other in the hospital's Quiet Room. If Dot's father had walked in, she'd have no idea who he was. She'd never met her father, or even seen a picture of him. Thea had always been very sketchy about that part of her life, which seemed to have happened shortly after she moved to Seattle from southern Indiana. Aunt Tab was already in Seattle; she was a reference librarian at the University of Washington. Thea had stayed with her sister only as long as

Two: Aunt Tab Appears

it took to get into college, find a part-time job, and rent someplace else to live.

Whenever Dot's father came up in conversation, which wasn't often, Thea would smile and call him "that tall guy from college" as if she didn't remember him well, but what she did remember was very pleasant. She didn't seem sad that he wasn't around, but she never said a single bad thing about him either.

Dot had been born on Christmas Day and Thea always said Dot was the best present anyone could ever imagine. She gave her daughter a long name: Dorothy Mary-Jane. She had her reasons.

Three: BT/AT

"Dorothy Mary-Jane, I have a plan." A few days after the funeral, Aunt Tab banged open Dot's bedroom door and strode in. Stepping over Dot's body, which was in its usual position shadowing Tinkerbell on the rug, Aunt Tab plopped down on Dot's messy bed. Dot remembered it had been Aunt Tab who had given her the Tinkerbell rug for her fifth birthday, saying how much they looked alike, both with short blonde hair and blue-green eyes.

It was the most attention Dot had ever received from her aunt, and she was as delighted as only a five-year-old who thinks the world is a truly wonderful place can be. For the rest of her kindergarten year, she ran around sprinkling imaginary pixie dust and granting wishes. In Dot's world, Tinkerbell didn't have a jealous fixation on anybody, and her pixie dust wasn't just about flying.

"We're going traveling," Aunt Tab barked, forcing Dot back to her horrible, motherless present. "England. You need this. I need this. Thea, wherever she may be, needs this."

Aunt Tab did not look upwards, as people often do when speaking of the dead, but glanced sharply around, as if she expected Thea to appear from behind Dot's bookshelf or to emerge from under the bed. Aunt Tab was turning out to have a spooky as well as a bossy side. Every evening, she set an extra place at the dinner table. "Hand the food around," Aunt Tab would order, and then it all ended up at the empty place.

Following Aunt Tab's abrupt and fidgety talk was nerve-wracking, like jumping from one dissolving ice floe to another. Thea, on the other hand, had always sounded like early morning mist rising from a mirror-clear mountain lake. Every word Thea said slipped into the next, her musical voice hanging in the scented air for ages. Listening to Thea was comforting; listening to Aunt Tab took work.

After Aunt Tab's trip announcement, Dot didn't move from her Tinkerbell position or take her eyes from her yellow wall. These days, which she labeled as **AT** or After the Truck, she was afraid of all moving objects, and didn't much want to move, herself. She was afraid to go outside; she was afraid of libraries and books, she was even afraid of clouds. She was pared down to the absolute basics—it took all her concentration to remember to alternate breathing in with breathing out.

Besides fighting through the horrible red memories, she also found **BT**—Before the Truck—scenes painful to remember, even though, or maybe especially because, they were all good. Tinkerbell was soaked in tears.

Dot's **BT** summertime memories were the best. Thea and Dot had always spent their summers together, roaming around Seattle, playing games and pretending to be different people. "A line is a dot that went for a walk," her mother used to say, pointing at street maps and bus routes. They'd ride the bus downtown and walk into an office building. They'd read through the list of businesses in the building, or if it had one of those touch-screen directories, they'd try different names at random. They took turns picking a business that sounded as if it weren't just a bunch of adults sitting at desks, and then they'd ride up the elevator for a visit. Dot would pretend she was doing a summer camp project, or Thea would say she was researching a magazine article and they had just a few questions to ask.

"People love to talk about themselves and their work," Thea had said, and it was true. Almost nobody turned them down. They'd been given a private tour of a dental crown-making lab, where they watched women in white coats and bright headlamps work with tiny instruments to shape bits of porcelain or gold into teeth that would exactly fit into someone's mouth. They'd visited the Library for the Blind where they listened to a woman reading from a cookbook for a local radio station. The reader told Dot that lots of blind people cook and they love to get new recipes from the radio.

Sometimes they'd walk south of downtown and poke around the International District. They visited the fortune cookie factory and the back rooms of the vegetable and fish markets where leafy vegetables were sorted, and still-flopping fish were hacked and filleted. Further south were factories that bent sheet metal into fireplace screens and milled ingots into boat cleats. They went through a deliciously aromatic bread bakery and a local dairy that made butter and ice cream. Dot and Thea took it all in, and there was never a test, they never had to write a paper or present a project. It was just for themselves, and all for fun.

But their best find ever was on a sunny second floor in a downtown high-rise. A huge open workroom was crowded with long tables piled high with giant books of fabric samples. Fashion sketches and swatches of colored fabrics covered the walls like graffiti, and the room buzzed with well-dressed, skinny people talking about silk and Milan. An employee named Sara gave Dot an armload of silk scraps in summer colors of bright orange and hot pink and ocean green. On the next dark and wet afternoon, Dot and her mother smoothed the silk out on the floor, cut it into coaster-sized pieces and arranged them into a grand collage. Then they crawled carefully over it, stitching the pieces together into a pattern so bright and wonderful it practically levitated off the floor.

"What do you see?" asked Thea.

"Everything. It's alive. It looks like happiness. I want to roll up in it and live forever."

Thea had laughed. "See the pictures?" She pointed at a green and white part. "There's a boat, a three-masted sailing ship tossing in a wide, green sea."

"Yeah," said Dot, getting into it. "And here's a house with lots of chimneys by an orange road."

"And it has a nice blue and yellow flower garden, too. Do you see anything else?"

"Another house. This one's smaller."

"Right. More like a cottage. And see, it's near a lake," Thea said, pointing to a nearby shiny blue patch.

Afterwards, Thea embroidered the words *Be Daring* on the middle sail of the boat, *Be Inventive* on the house with the chimneys and the flower garden, and *Be Loyal* on the cottage by the lake. Dot read them out:

Be Daring
Be Inventive
Be Loyal

"What's that about, Mom?"

"Different ways of being—each one is good by itself, but a happy, useful life really needs all three. They go together. You'll see. It's about your name, too: Dorothy Mary-Jane."

"I don't get it."

"It's complicated." She caught her daughter in a happy hug and led her in a dance around the edges of the patterned silk collage. "Don't worry, it can wait."

Thea was right about the complexity, but she was wrong that it could wait.

They christened the collage *Dancing on the Edge*. "Because that's what life is," said Thea. "The best parts, anyway."

Later in the afternoon, Thea hung *Dancing on the Edge* on the wall next to the shelf of her poetry books—Wordsworth, Coleridge, Shelley. "I love those guys," Thea said to Dot, running her hand across the spines of the books. "They rearranged poetry like nobody's business. Rearranging things is as close to creation as people ever get. Even people are just rearrangements of DNA—we're our own best creation."

When Dot tried to read Thea's poetry books, she couldn't make much sense of them. Some of the poems were about daffodils and pretty scenery, and some were scary descriptions of being followed down lonely roads by fearsome Monsters (writers in those days used a lot of capital letters), and others seemed to be about politics. But she loved *Dancing on the Edge* and she loved the way her mother's words, no matter what the subject, always promised lots of wonderful exploring yet to be done.

• • •

When the *Dancing on the Edge* memory came, Dot's brain worked extra hard at destroying trucks. She was spending her **AT** waking hours (and there were a lot of them because sleep wasn't coming so easily) either swamped in these happy yet terrible memories or developing her patented Explosivision so that every truck she so much as glanced at would explode into smithereens. Most of the truck drivers wouldn't survive either—if they had families, too bad for them.

"A trip!" Aunt Tab repeated, prodding Dot's hunched shoulder, "It's just the thing."

"I think I'll just stay here, Aunt Tab," said Dot, locking herself more firmly into her Tinkerbell position and hooking her eyes to nearby tufts of blue yarn.

"Not a chance. That rug needs a wash, and so do you. Don't want to miss our plane. I wonder how much ash they'll let us carry on. A trip! That's the ticket." Aunt Tab laughed, more like a rusty croak, at her lame pun.

Dot slowly unglued her arms from her sides and rolled onto her back. Turning her head, she saw that Aunt Tab was now perched on the purple corduroy beanbag chair by her bookshelf. She really did look like a flamingo. An irritating flamingo sitting on a giant purple egg. It occurred to Dot that she could smile at that, but smiling belonged to a different Dot in a different world, long ago, in **BT** time.

"I. Do. Not. Want. To. Go. Anywhere. With. You." said Dot, enunciating slowly and clearly. Then she added, "What about school?" She threw this in because she knew grown-ups generally didn't like kids to miss school, not because she personally cared about school anymore. She hadn't been back to school since that trip to the library and she knew she'd never return. She didn't even care if she never saw her favorite teacher Mr. Cyrus again. I'll just stay here forever and be a hermit, she thought. Or maybe I'll run away.

Four: A Failed Try

Although Aunt Tab had sounded so urgent, their plane wasn't for another three weeks. Once Dot got that figured out, she didn't expect the trip to happen at all. **AT** time, she'd noticed, didn't act like **BT** time. **AT** time was elastic and squishy, and didn't go forward in the predictable way it had in **BT**. In **AT** days, time kept looping back and getting stuck and then jumping every which way. It made her dizzy. Better to stay anchored on Tinkerbell.

A week before they were supposed to leave, Dot's wandering mind was interrupted by her best friend Junie. Junie was in Dot's homeroom at Susan B. Anthony Middle School and they'd been friends since third grade at Louisa May Alcott Elementary School. Dot couldn't have said why she and Junie became best friends, but it might have been because Junie had Thea's way of seeing a good side, at least a *potential* good side, to everything. Like when Junie got her braces, which were torturously large and industrial-looking, she'd laughed and said her Frankenstein grin came in handy when she babysat her brothers and had to scare them into brushing their teeth and getting ready for bed.

Junie wore cheerful brown braids, which were totally not acceptable in middle school, with different colored ribbons tied at the end of each one. Sometimes the ribbons matched her mismatched socks and sometimes they didn't.

Junie ran up the stairs to Dot's room and sat on the floor next to the Tinkerbell rug. She chewed on the end of a braid as she looked at her friend.

"Let's go outside."

Four: A Failed Try

Dot could practically hear Junie's black eyes snapping.

"No."

"It's sunny. You should open your curtains."

"No."

"We miss you at school. Mr. Cyrus told us all about your mom. Everybody's real sad. We all put notes on Facebook for you." Junie poked Dot's arm with a gentle finger.

"So?" Dot stared hard at the tufts of blue near her face, thinking about Mr. Cyrus and his history class. "I hate history," she realized that very second. What had history ever done for her? It was about things that happened to dead people and nothing good could ever come from that. As for Facebook, forget it. A few days ago, in a moment of inspired desperation, she'd posted a note on Thea's Facebook page, just in case. She'd checked it yesterday. Nothing.

Junie tried a different tack. "Your Aunt Tab says you're going on a trip."

"I told her no."

"She says you're going to England. That's a whole other country. You need a passport. They take your picture."

Dot took her eyes off the blue yarn and looked at Junie. So that's what that picture-taking down at the Copy & Print had been about. It was the first time she'd been outside since the funeral. Aunt Tab had hustled her down the street—Dot cringing, terrified, on the inside of the sidewalk, far away from the curb. At least Aunt Tab wasn't making her ride the bus. Dot knew she'd never be able to stand at a bus stop again. When they reached Aunt Tab's dirty blue Prius, Dot waited until Aunt Tab pulled the passenger door wide open before she was willing to sprint across the sidewalk toward the street. She fought off her nausea by blowing up all nearby vehicles, red or not, with her Explosivision.

When the clerk gave them their pictures, Dot looked completely freaked out. She was, so much so that she never got around to asking Aunt Tab why they'd had them taken.

"How do you know about passports?"

"My parents went to Africa once, before I was born. I've seen the pictures. Lions and elephants and stuff. Anyway, they had to go through England and they said you can see icebergs and the Northern Lights."

"In England?" Dot was on the verge of a smile. Junie did that to her.

"No, silly. From the plane—it flies practically over the North Pole to get from Seattle to England."

Dot felt even a tiny bit better when Junie called her silly. It felt normal.

"Okay, maybe. But just the backyard." Dot rolled off Tinkerbell and stood up carefully. Junie was already halfway down the stairs. "Good!" she yelled back.

Thea and Dot had moved into their house eight years ago, and Junie's family was already living next door. Their houses were called skinny houses because they were tall and thin enough to build two side by side on a regular-sized city lot. Thea said it was a huge plus that you had to run up and down a lot of steep stairs to get anywhere.

When they'd moved in, all the walls were white and there was beige carpeting everywhere. Thea painted the walls all different colors and laid bright rugs from Ikea on top of the boring carpet. The rugs were islands of color all over the house—perfect for jumping over or setting up camps and forts on. But it was different now; **AT** had darkened everything. She used to love her house and now she didn't.

Downstairs, the girls found Aunt Tab cross-legged on an orange rug in the living room, reading travel books about England and taking notes on lined yellow paper.

"We're going out," Junie said, checking to make sure Dot had caught up with her. Aunt Tab looked up and didn't say a thing about this being the first time Dot was going out of her own free will since that terrible trip to the library.

"Be back in an hour," Aunt Tab said. "Bangers and mash for dinner. Strange foods those English eat. Spotted Dick—can't imagine what that is. And fries are chips and chips are crisps. And milk in tea. Much to learn,

Four: A Failed Try

much to learn." She pushed her curly graying hair off her forehead, as if that would give her brain more space for absorbing English oddities.

"Okay, Aunt Tab," Dot said, wondering briefly what would happen if Aunt Tab went completely bonkers. Running away might become the only sensible option.

But when she reached the front door, Dot remembered sidewalks and trucks. "Maybe I won't go," she said to Junie and pulled her hand away from the door knob.

"C'mon, Dot. You can't stay inside forever."

"You're not my mother!" Dot turned her back on her friend and stomped upstairs.

Aunt Tab craned herself off the floor, shedding maps and guidebooks as she walked over to give Junie a pat on the back. "Might have to drag her by her ears to get her to the airport." Aunt Tab grinned in such a lopsided way that Junie couldn't tell if she was joking or not.

Five: Packing What Matters

"Time to pack. We leave in an hour." Aunt Tab spoke from her full and imposing height to curled-up Dot on her Tinkerbell rug.

"No," said Dot, as defiantly as possible for a person lying on a rug. "I'm not going."

"Yes, you are. Thea wants us to."

"You can't talk with Mom."

"You'd be surprised." It sounded like a threat.

After more back and forth like this, which got nowhere, Aunt Tab creaked down, fork-lifted Dot to a standing position and didn't let go. Being upright, Dot could see a brand new suitcase open on her bed. She also noticed that all her clothing drawers were pulled open.

"Pick out what you want to wear in England. We'll be there seven days. It will be sunny some days and rainy some days, just like here." Aunt Tab had a take-no-prisoners look in her beady eyes. "You have twenty minutes to make your choices and fill your bag. Don't get greedy and fill it all up because you might want to bring some new stuff home."

"Aunt Tab," Dot started in a whiney voice, twisting her arm to get out of Aunt Tab's bony grasp.

"Don't you Aunt Tab me, young lady. This is one of those times when the kid has to do what the grown-up says. Pack. Now."

Aunt Tab had that unyielding look that Thea never had.

"Okay," Dot mumbled. "But I don't want to go and I'm not going to have any fun."

Five: Packing What Matters

"Don't worry. This trip isn't a vacation for either of us." Aunt Tab looked grim. "Enough talk—pack!" She let go of Dot's arm and waited, hands on her skinny hips, to make sure Dot wasn't about to crumple back down on Tinkerbell. Satisfied, she turned and loped out of the bedroom.

Dot stared at her new suitcase. It was dark green and covered with zippers. The curve of one of the zippers looked a little like Junie's braces when she smiled. Dot didn't smile back. She picked up Tinkerbell and carefully laid the rug in the suitcase and then tossed in a sweatshirt and a couple pairs of jeans. In a few minutes, the suitcase was full. But no books, shoes, socks, underwear or tee shirts had made it in. Dot took everything out and stared at Tinkerbell. Silly to think she would fit; still, it was worse to think of leaving her home.

After some thought, Dot remembered the sharp fabric scissors in Thea's sewing basket. Maybe she could cut Tinkerbell out and leave her bulky blue background at home. This seemed like a good idea until she realized she would have to go into her mother's room to get the sewing basket, which was on the floor of her mother's closet.

Dot hadn't been in Thea's room since Thea stopped being there.

She walked down the short hallway and stood at her mother's closed bedroom door for a while. She could hear Aunt Tab crashing around in the kitchen downstairs, and above her a jet decelerated over her neighborhood, headed to Sea-Tac Airport to the south. A dog barked down the street. Everything sounded echoey and mechanical as AT time jerked to a halt. In slow motion she reached for the bedroom doorknob. She touched it with one finger, half expecting an electric shock. Nothing—just cold metal. She wrapped her warm hand around the knob, gently turned it, and pushed the door open.

The air in the room that rushed out to greet Dot smelled like Thea. She leaned against the door frame and shut her eyes against alternating waves of sweetness and pain. She couldn't stop herself from taking a deep breath and holding in the air of her past. When she finally exhaled, she cautiously cracked her eyes open, just to a narrow slit, and forced herself to walk in.

The room looked exactly as it had the morning they'd set off for the library. Her mother's orange terrycloth bathrobe was flung like a sunset across the bottom of her rumpled blue duvet. There were piles of books on the floor on both sides at the head of the bed. The closet door was half open. Dot realized Aunt Tab hadn't been in there either. She moved cautiously toward the closet.

She found the sewing basket mostly by feel. Without taking it out and with her eyes still mostly shut, she opened it, retrieved the scissors and ran out of the room, eyes pricked with tears as she pulled the door closed.

She couldn't imagine ever going back in. She couldn't imagine sorting through her mother's things, getting rid of things, turning the room into something else. But then she thought it would be creepy to leave it as it was, knowing it would eventually crumble into spider webs and dust.

No good choices, just like everything else in her life these days.

Back in her own room, Dot was glad to focus on the physical labor of cutting out Tinkerbell. It was trickier than she expected and took all her strength and attention. The rug material was much tougher than any fabric the scissors were made for, and it was hard to follow Tinkerbell's outstretched arm and the skinny wand. But eventually it was done, and Tinkerbell fit nicely into the bottom of the suitcase.

Now there was plenty of room. She stuffed in the clothes she wanted and saw she still had room left. She went downstairs and took the fabric collage *Dancing on the Edge* from the wall next to Thea's poetry shelf. Rolled tightly, it slid neatly along one side, next to her jeans. After a wave of bittersweet **BT** memories, she zipped the suitcase closed and dragged it down the stairs. Might as well get it over with.

Part II: Destinations & Detours

Six: A Terrible Start

The inside of the airplane was huge. Dot had seen airplane insides only on TV, so she was impressed by the size of the real thing. It was frighteningly big. Bumping her suitcase down the aisle (Aunt Tab said she didn't believe in checking bags), she was convinced it could never stay up in the air. By the time they'd walked the mile or so to their seats, Dot became equally convinced that it would never be able to take off and that they'd all end up in a fiery ball at the end of the runway.

The rows of seats went on forever, each row nine seats across with two aisles. Dot and Aunt Tab's tickets put them in two adjacent seats in the five-seat middle section—Aunt Tab in the aisle seat and Dot one seat in. Aunt Tab's skinny arms were pretty strong and she put their bags in a sliding compartment above their seats by herself, even though a man across the aisle offered to help.

Dot sat down and expected the plane to start immediately lumbering down the runway to its certain destruction. When it didn't, she fiddled with the light switches on her arm rest and watched people fight over the diminishing space in the overhead compartments. After that got boring, she looked across the empty seat beside her and saw two kids, a girl and a boy, sit down in the two seats on the other side of her row. They looked about her age, maybe a year older, and they didn't seem to have any adults attached to them. They were each wearing black hoodie sweatshirts with "Microsoft Computer Camp" printed in red, green, yellow, and blue down their left arms. Except for the red, Dot had to admit they were pretty cool sweatshirts.

Six: A Terrible Start

The two kids appeared to know everything about the little buttons and lights around their seats. They were also bickering noisily about something and fighting over a pillow.

"Oh, hello there," the girl interrupted her squabble as she noticed Dot looking at her.

"Hi," said Dot, as noncommittally as possible. Making new friends was not high on her list, because then she'd have to talk about stuff.

"Are you American?" the girl asked. She had an English accent.

"Yes." Dot looked at Aunt Tab, hoping she'd join in and scare them off or at least take over the conversation. But Aunt Tab wasn't paying attention; she'd gotten up and was rearranging bags overhead so someone else could cram his stuff in.

"I'm Nell. This is my brother Nick. We're twins and we've been to computer camp in Seattle. We're English and we're going home." Nell pushed her dark curly hair behind her ears and Dot noticed her brother had the same hair, even the same length. They both had bright blue eyes and light pink skin.

"I'm Dot. That's my Aunt Tab." Dot stopped. She had no idea what to say next; no idea how to explain why she was going to England. She didn't even know herself. Aunt Tab's explanations had been scattershot, as usual, and even if Dot had paid attention, which she hadn't, they probably wouldn't have made sense. Something about ashes and something about the meaning of Dot's name *Dorothy Mary-Jane*, which apparently was complicated and meaningful—she vaguely remembered her mother telling her the same thing, but it hadn't stuck. Whatever the reasons, they didn't matter anymore. Nothing in **AT** time mattered. Besides, none of this was simple small talk for when you meet a kid for the first time.

Dot wished Junie were there. She'd know what to say. She'd flip her braids at them and spout off something about Chinese pirates stealing terabytes of Microsoft software. Junie always sounded as if she knew what she was talking about, even when she didn't.

Dot began feeling extremely sorry for herself—missing her mother and now missing her best friend. How could Aunt Tab possibly think this trip was a good idea?

Dot was rescued from having to think of what to say to the English kids when a woman in a uniform started a long speech on ceiling-mounted video screens about what to do if the plane began to crash. Good, thought Dot, I'm not the only one who's worried. Then she noticed that no one else was paying any attention, which she thought probably meant that none of the instructions would make any difference. Even so, she double-checked her seat belt when the video got to that part.

Taking off was a slow and undramatic process. Aunt Tab was restive because she couldn't see out a window. "No good at all. Like being in a shipping container."

About an hour into the flight, Dot almost forgot that she was in a thin and fragile tube with only miles of icy air between her and a very rocky, completely non-bouncy surface. A little while later, a sort of dinner was passed out. Dot didn't eat much. There was a tiny lettuce salad with one hard cherry tomato and a piece of chicken covered in a gooey something and a stale roll and a few green beans. She picked at a chocolate cupcake that was drizzled with a sticky sauce that tasted like damp brown sugar.

"So why are you going to England?" Nick asked from across the empty seat as he finished his last bite of beans. He said it like it was a challenge, not friendly at all.

"It's about my mom." Dot didn't know any other way to begin. "She died, and..." Dot turned to Aunt Tab, hoping for help.

"Well, hello, you young people," said Aunt Tab, smiling as benevolently as she probably knew how. Surprised and relieved, Dot stuffed a big piece of cake into her mouth so she wouldn't have to talk for a while.

"Yes, my niece Dot and I are visiting your fair country. I take it from your accents that you are of British stock," she waved a gloppy forkful of chicken in their direction, "We plan to partake of your literal and literary landscapes—"

"Your mother died?" Nick interrupted, looking at Dot. "So you're spending her insurance money or what?"

Six: A Terrible Start

Dot was so stunned by Nick's nastiness that she wished she could disappear into the seat pocket in front of her. Either that or leap across the empty seat between them and hit his head as hard as a speeding truck.

"Young man! Did your mother never teach you a modicum of manners?" Aunt Tab bristled in a very satisfying way and stretched her arm across Dot's seat to shake a bony finger at Nick.

Nick ignored Aunt Tab and turned to his sister, "Nell, the empty seat is for that girl's mother. She's a ghost."

"Nick, stop bothering them," Nell said in a tired voice and swatted her brother's arm.

"Travel does not come without risks," Aunt Tab muttered. "Dot, let's change seats."

"Let's just go home," Dot trembled. "We never should've left."

"Come, come. We don't crumple that easily. Put your tray on the empty seat between you and that execrable young man, and then you get up and hold my tray and then I'll get up and then we'll change seats and when I sit down in your seat you can give me my tray and then when you sit down in my seat, I'll give you your tray. Hang on to your pillow and keep that blanket off the floor. Simple."

"I get the picture, Aunt Tab. I'm not stupid."

Despite the clear plan, Aunt Tab spilled Dot's salad container on the floor. Aunt Tab was as uncoordinated as Thea had been graceful.

"Dreadful children," she said to Dot when they'd finally been rearranged, "Not representative, we must assume, of Great Britain's finest."

Dot stared straight ahead into the blue fabric seatback in front of her and didn't answer. The color reminded her of the part of the Tinkerbell rug she'd left behind, carefully folded and tucked under her bed. It had begun to appear that the plane might make it all the way to London, so it was good she'd brought Tink with her. And *Dancing on the Edge*:

Be Daring
Be Inventive
Be Loyal.

Was there any help there? Not that she could see. Not yet.

After the dinner trays were collected, the attendants turned out the lights and most people started wiggling around in their seats, trying to find a sitting-up position where they might possibly fall asleep.

"When you wake up, we'll be in London," said Aunt Tab. "First stop: Mary Wollstonecraft."

"Whatever," said Dot, perfectly resigned to a terrible week. It certainly had started out that way.

Seven: Soup's On

"Thank goodness we didn't check luggage," Aunt Tab said as they strolled right through the crush of people waiting at London's Heathrow Airport for their bags. "People take the wrong suitcases all the time. Like a white elephant exchange. Never know what you'll get."

London's Heathrow Airport looked to Dot's sleep-deprived eyes like a city-sized mall with thousands of tired people pushing their suitcases around in huge shopping carts. The travelers were dressed in clothes from all over the world—saris, turbans, flowing robes, headscarves. She saw college students in hiking gear, businessmen in pin-striped three-piece suits and soldiers in camouflage and berets. She and Aunt Tab rolled their suitcases past restaurants jammed with people eating fried fish and Chinese dumplings and pasta and oysters. People jabbered in a dozen languages and it seemed to be every time of day at once. It was confusing. Suddenly nervous, she looked back at her suitcase, worried that its zippers had failed and maybe Tink had fallen out.

When she turned around, Dot spotted nasty Nick and his sister Nell standing alone with a mountain of suitcases, looking annoyed. All around them were other people's families and friends greeting each other, hugging and laughing. Nell looked as if she might burst into tears. Then she and Nick started arguing with each other.

"They're never here," Dot heard Nell say.

"Of course not. What did you expect?" Nick responded. "Never mind, we'll get a taxi."

Dot thought taxis were incredibly exotic, and said so to Aunt Tab, who agreed.

Seven: Soup's On

"Not for us *hoi polloi*. We're taking the Tube—the Piccadilly Line—love British words. *Tube* is so much better than *subway*. Wonder what Piccadilly means—a circus of acrobatic pickles?" She cackled and added spookily, "Your mother's loving this."

"Stop it, Aunt Tab." Dot's voice sounded as tired and disheartened as Nell's.

Despite Aunt Tab's guidebooks and maps, they had trouble finding the airport Tube station, and then when they boarded the train, they had to stand up for most of the hour-long ride into London. At first their car was crowded with other travelers and their suitcases, and as they got closer to town, even more local people crammed in. These Londoners, reading or talking or staring into space, were as varied as the people at the airport. Dot had to admit that seeing these different people all sharing this cramped space as they went about their business was exactly the sort of experience her mother would have appreciated.

When the tracks ran above ground, Dot watched rows of connected houses fly by, each with tiled roofs and narrow backyards draped with laundry and planted with flowers and spring vegetables. The concrete retaining walls next to the tracks were covered with colorful graffiti shaped exactly like the graffiti in Seattle. Some letters were puffy and some sharply angular, outlined and shaded in certain ways, as if there were only a few approved graffiti fonts that every tagger in the world had to use.

When they arrived at their stop, called Piccadilly Circus, Aunt Tab and Dot wrestled their bags up several flights of dirty, crowded stairs. "Popping up like prairie dogs," Aunt Tab said, as they emerged on the west side of a heavily trafficked circular intersection. There was no tent or Ferris wheel, or pickles, for that matter. Instead, Dot blinked at a bronze statue of a naked boy with wings who was shooting a bow and arrow into the sky. He was in a center island, surrounded by honking, bumper-to-bumper traffic and pedestrian mayhem. Turning away from the scary traffic, she saw a music store named Virgin (in big red letters), and on the other side of the naked boy statue was a building studded with plaster statues of rock stars, some with red guitars. Huge neon signs in red and blue ringed the sidewalks, which were choked with vendors selling newspapers, postcards, flags (more red), candy and bottled water. The streets were crowded with red buses.

So much red was bad, very bad; Dot's stomach flipped and she had to look down at her green Converse sneakers and make herself breathe to keep from throwing up. When she cautiously raised her head again and peeked around, she shielded her eyes with her free hand whenever a red splotch motored into view. So many horrible blood-red buses made it hard for her to look at the streets. Clearly, she'd have to expand her Explosivision work to include buses as well as trucks.

Even in her fear and nausea, Dot noticed that the traffic moved on opposite sides of the street from Seattle. She thought about mentioning it to Aunt Tab, especially when she realized that if the truck had been coming from the other direction, then her mother wouldn't be dead. Maybe England had a few good points, after all.

But just as she thought about warming up to the place, a whole convoy of trucks with big side-view mirrors came around the traffic circle. Dot went ice cold and flattened herself tight against the music store window, behind Aunt Tab, who was studying her maps to find the way to their hotel.

"We go north, young lady," Aunt Tab said, not noticing Dot's paralysis and abruptly starting across Piccadilly Street, not looking in the right direction for the oncoming traffic.

"Hey, Aunt Tab!" Through a haze of fear, Dot saw oncoming tragedy and lunged to grab her aunt away from a honking, screeching taxi.

"Thank you, my dear." Aunt Tab straightened her jacket and patted her suitcase as she returned to the sidewalk. "Goodness me, almost an orphan all over again."

"Watch it, will you?" Dot said angrily.

They crossed the street carefully, looking in every possible direction, and threaded their way along Shaftsbury Street to Greek Street into a neighborhood called Soho. Dot hugged the buildings, avoiding the curb as if it were the lip of the Grand Canyon. Aunt Tab, fully recovered, started

Seven: Soup's On

blabbing on and on about how Piccadilly had been an important intersection for centuries and quite likely Mary Wollstonecraft had strode along this very street when she lived here in the late 1700s, and when Jane Austen and Dorothy Wordsworth had visited from their quiet rural homes, they had most certainly walked here, too.

The flow of names—Dorothy Wordsworth, Mary Wollstonecraft, Jane Austen—reminded Dot of what Aunt Tab had said at the kitchen table a week ago, about how Dot's names were the reason for this England trip. They'd sat down to a dinner of fried eggs and peanut butter toast when Aunt Tab said, "I suppose your mother may not have gotten around to telling you the story of your names."

Dot poked her toast into her runny egg yolks and said, "She did so."

Aunt Tab had managed to cook the eggs exactly as Dot liked them, and, until Aunt Tab said that about her mother, Dot was toying with the idea of actually eating a bite or two.

Of course Thea had told her who she was named after, undoubtedly she did, but Dot had to admit (to herself, certainly not to Aunt Tab) that she'd mostly forgotten it. Thea had talked about naming Dot as if it were a story with the three women characters, and there was a plot and even a Monster. Then Thea had said the story didn't have a clear ending, which made Dot impatient, and so she lost interest.

"These three women mattered, and not just to your mother." The London traffic noise was so loud that Aunt Tab, marching ahead, had to shout back at Dot as they made their way up Greek Street. Dot was falling behind, clinging to storefronts and walls. She felt like a lost squirrel on the windy ledge of a skyscraper.

"Dorothy Wordsworth, Mary Wollstonecraft and Jane Austen all lived in England about two hundred years ago—Dorothy north of London, Mary in London and Jane south of London. Very different lives but grappling with the same problems. Not so different from today, really. That's why we're here," Aunt Tab shouted as if it all made perfect sense. "Dorothy Mary-Jane."

36

Of course it didn't make sense. But this time that lack of sense created a tiny tickle of interest in Dot's brain, like a shake of pixie dust had suddenly filled the London air she was breathing. Dot remembered her mother saying that the pictures in *Dancing on the Edge*—the boat and the two houses, and their inscriptions—had something to do with the three women Dot was named after.

Be Daring
Be Inventive
Be Loyal

But it was complicated, and now Dot was tired and it's hard to care about three women who'd been dead for two hundred years when your own mother has been dead less than two months and you weren't too sure about the point of staying alive yourself. Keeping up with Aunt Tab's long strides on the busy London sidewalk was also increasingly tricky, especially having to maneuver a suitcase along the crowded and cracked sidewalk, stay safely away from the deadly curb, and still manage to aim and blow up red moving objects.

When Dot and Aunt Tab had dragged their suitcases for five difficult blocks, they passed a small lunch café with a hand-painted sandwich-board sign outside saying "Soup's On." Wonderful savory smells came from the open door.

"Let's eat," Aunt Tab said, feeling in her pocket for the pounds (funny name for dollars, Dot thought) she had gotten from an ATM at the airport. They went inside, dodging their bags around the tiny tables to join a cafeteria line at the back.

"The World Cup of soup," Aunt Tab said as she read the labels on the caldrons: Chinese noodle soup, Scottish beef and barley, Italian minestrone, African peanut stew, chicken noodle, green lamb curry. Two women were ladling soup into large white bowls and handing them to customers along with a plate of crusty, grainy bread and a small salad of greens,

Seven: Soup's On

radishes, and cucumbers. The self-serve dessert shelf at the end of the counter was crowded with puddings and pastries in garish reds, yellows, and purples.

Dot took a small bowl of plain-looking chicken noodle soup and shielded her eyes from the red desserts. Aunt Tab chose the chunky minestrone and a wobbly yellow dessert pock-marked with nuts and raisins.

They sat down at a rickety table crowded close to a table occupied by three women dressed in very old-fashioned clothing with lots of bits to keep track of: bonnets, shawls, gloves, handkerchiefs, ribbons, vests, skirts, parasols. Everything they wore had multiple layers that were buttoned or pinned or tied in fussy, difficult ways. It must have taken a lot of work to get dressed in the old days, Dot thought as she noticed them, and wondered if they were on a break from acting in a movie.

At first glance, the three women looked very much alike with their hair pinned up in waves under bonnets and ribbons. They appeared to be in their twenties or early thirties. Looking more carefully, though, Dot could see differences. The first woman was the most attractive, probably between the other two in age, and had large dark eyes and thick curly hair. She was dressed in sky blue and maroon, and although she seemed the most at ease with the urban scene, she had a shadowy, convalescing look about her.

The second woman was the youngest of the three. She was dressed in lilac and peach colors and was the only one who glanced around, smiling, from time to time, as if she greatly enjoyed being in the hubbub of the crowded restaurant.

The third one was dressed in dark brown wool that was patched around the hem. This woman looked a little uneasy, as if city crowds unnerved her. She also grimaced frequently as if in pain and Dot noticed she was drinking large amounts of hot tea.

As Aunt Tab was eating and being unexpectedly quiet, Dot couldn't help overhearing the women's conversation. It was just the sort of peeking-into-other-people's-lives opportunity that Thea would have wanted her to have.

Eight: Eavesdropping on Enlightenment

"I am so pleased to be here. My brothers do not approve of my coming to London. I am running away, if only for a visit," the youngest woman, wearing lilac and peach, said as she pushed her bonnet back from her face and looked eagerly around. She seemed delighted and energized by the hustle and bustle of the busy café. Glancing down at her companions' empty teacups, she murmured "Oh my!" and poured out another round.

"Thank you, yes," said the dark-eyed one with the convalescing look, as she reached for her filled teacup. "I am very glad for our little party and grateful for the invitation. I am not so sure I could have recovered, even partially, from my relentless melancholy, let alone my desperate leap into the unforgiving river, without the kindness of friends such as yourselves."

If the two other ladies were surprised to hear about a desperate leap into an unforgiving river, they didn't show it. Dot, though, was startled. Although her own life had become so pointless and miserable that spending the rest of it lying on her bedroom floor seemed a reasonable option, ending it altogether hadn't occurred to her. And yet here were these three over-dressed women drinking tea and chatting calmly about suicidal leaps into unforgiving rivers.

The first woman, the dark-eyed one, went on, "The catastrophes of my life temporarily overwhelmed me that night on the bridge. I believe myself now much improved, and ready to return to this chaotic city. I have traveled too far, and for too long. Do you know my story?" She impatiently tucked her unruly dark hair behind her ears as she looked at her companions.

Eight: Eavesdropping on Enlightenment

"Let me tell you and my despair will be diminished, I am sure, by this lovely day and our pleasant luncheon."

"Oh, please do not speak if it troubles you, Miss Wollstonecraft," replied the youngest woman, adjusting her bonnet again and pouring more tea for their third companion. "Begging your pardon for speaking frankly, but much as I love stories, I find tales of great personal tragedy both upsetting and unnecessarily tedious, and this day is made for neither."

The woman with the patches on her brown skirts spoke with a slight stammer and stumbled over the hard consonants. "Thank you so much, Miss Austen. The warmth of the tea much improves my aching gums. I will be seeing the dentist later this afternoon, but in the meantime, I will counter your preferences with the hope that Miss Wollstonecraft's story will distract me from my current, personal pain. So, if you are comfortable with the telling, please proceed. I am sure Miss Austen, for all her youth, can modulate her auditory capacities to admit only what she pleases."

Dot, blatantly listening, agreed wholeheartedly with the woman in brown. She definitely wanted to hear the story. As she adjusted to the more complicated sentences the women were speaking, she liked the way they sounded.

"I appreciate your forthright speech, Miss Wordsworth," began the dark-eyed one called Miss Wollstonecraft. "Although my troubles may appear to be personal, Miss Austen, they are but a desperate reflection of our political chaos. Our pampered aristocracy trembles in its dancing shoes, afraid (and rightfully, I sincerely hope) that England shall be the third nation, after America and France, to topple its useless King. All around us the fearful rich are reacting with force—closing newspapers, prohibiting public gatherings, arresting hundreds. Our friends are being jailed! Executions daily! Bread prices are inflated out of reach—families are torn asunder; mothers and babes, as always, suffering cruelly!"

Miss Wordsworth, continuing to swish tea around the inside of her left cheek, nodded firmly, saying something about Mr. Coleridge speaking out against the aristocracy, saying treason and terror were being committed by the government, not by the people. Miss Austen pulled on her bonnet ribbons and murmured something about sharing food with needy families in her village, and then added, "Perhaps, Miss Wollstonecraft, I will soften my objection to hearing your *personal* story, as I care even less for polemics and politics. So please, tell us about your *own* circumstances." She quickly scanned the café as she spoke, and surprised Dot by looking straight at her and giving her a gentle smile.

"Very well, Miss Austen, but I do not endorse your position on the irrelevance of politics." She sighed and continued, "Here, then, is the personal: A fortnight ago, in that dreadful storm, I made my way to Putney Bridge, pelted by rain and whipped by the night wind. From the middle of the bridge, the River Thames below was as dark and as discomposed as my own mind. I paced back and forth waiting for my clothing to become heavy with rainwater. I was shot through with the agony of leaving my darling baby Fanny, a child of the Revolution, but could see only blackness in my present or future. I could endure it no longer. Looking at my unhappy world one last time, I jumped into the cold arms of the waiting river."

Miss Wollstonecraft paused to slurp her tea. Her combination of sincerity and high theatre reminded Dot of her mother. At the same time, Dot couldn't understand how this pretty, lively woman could ever choose death, especially if she had a baby daughter. She had a strong urge to move over to their table and join the conversation. She looked at Aunt Tab, who was eating and studying her maps, oblivious to the whole scene.

"Don't you see that?" Dot asked her, pointing at the three ladies' table.

"What?" Aunt Tab looked around, obviously seeing and hearing nothing out of the ordinary.

Weird, though Dot, and then was immediately drawn back to eavesdropping by Miss Austen's exclamation, "How terrible for you, Miss Wollstonecraft! I shudder to imagine how abandoned you must have felt."

Miss Austen spoke with such warm and comforting understanding that Dot immediately wanted to tell her about the sidewalk in front of the library. "Abandonment," Miss Wordsworth mused, holding her warm

Eight: Eavesdropping on Enlightenment

teacup against her left cheek for a moment, "When I was orphaned and separated from my brothers, I felt unutterably lost, but never driven to self-destruction." She smoothed the rough country fabric of her pelisse, as if it reminded her of tough times. "But, Miss Wollstonecraft, you have survived, thank the Lord. What drove you to such despair? And what saved you?"

"Miss Wordsworth, you ask difficult questions." She sat up straighter. "I have tried to pursue justice and progress in all things. It is a solitary struggle for a woman, this battle for a better, more equal life," she raised her hands as if in defeat, "and I was beaten. Beaten and betrayed. Even the man I loved failed me." Fanning herself with a large handkerchief, Miss Wollstonecraft stopped briefly.

Dot snuck another look at Aunt Tab, who was still eating, apparently seeing or hearing none of this. What was going on?

"I was not, however, allowed to rest at the bottom of the river," Miss Wollstonecraft said, picking up her story. "Fate decreed that my plunge was witnessed, and two fishermen pulled me from the dark waters, and following new medical advice, breathed life back into my cold and helpless body. I knew not whether to curse them or thank them. Apparently I must live. I must continue the fight. This time, I am determined to overcome my devils. I will not let my heart and my strength be undermined again."

She firmly replaced a curl that had escaped her cap and ran the back of her hand across her eyes before darting a glance directly at Dot and Aunt Tab's table, saying pointedly, "We nourish our better selves when we struggle against the injustices of our world. That is reason enough to take the next breath."

"Your book, *A Vindication of the Rights of Woman,* is indeed a bold and feisty volume," replied Miss Wordsworth. "Daring to struggle can indeed strengthen us. But even the lead bird must drop back from time to time. To maintain your degree of effort must be most exhausting," said Miss Wordsworth, rubbing her cheek again with her warm teacup and looking a bit exhausted herself.

"*Vindication of the Rights of Woman* is such an angry book," Miss Austen said quietly. "Well-reasoned, but angry. I prefer a lighter touch.

The sordid difficulties of life are always with us; why bring them into our books? My family does not agree with the excesses of democracy such as we have seen across the Channel in France. If the guillotine were to come to London—"

"Ah, Miss Austen, I see you follow politics after all. But please do not confuse my call for the rights of women or the fall of the monarchy with the horrors of those endless French beheadings," Miss Wollstonecraft interrupted. "The Terror there, the Revolution gone awry, has chilled me deeply, for I traveled to Paris to see it firsthand. Returning to my *atelier* one evening, I walked across the slippery mud of the Champs du Mars, and only when I arrived home did I realize that my hems were soaked not with muddy rainwater, but with blood. The guillotines had been especially busy that day. I added my tears to the wash tub that evening."

Fighting to ignore the reference to blood, Dot tried to remember if Mr. Cyrus's history class had covered any of this. She was pretty sure he'd said something about there having been a French Revolution and that it hadn't worked out as well as the American one. That must be what they were talking about.

"Travel carries such awful risks," Miss Austen murmured quietly. So true, thought Dot, wanting to add that you don't even have to leave your hometown to have something terrible happen.

"We all need a purpose in our lives," Miss Wollstonecraft continued, "else we will drift through our precious time here on this earth with nothing to show for it. I am impatient with those who do not work to improve the horrendous state of our world."

"You do have a frank way of speaking, Miss Wollstonecraft," said Miss Austen, refilling Miss Wordsworth's always empty tea cup. "In the stories I am thinking about writing, there are so many sides to every problem; my best characters need to think for themselves. Life is an intricate tapestry, though, and mistakes will always be made. My favorite characters eventually learn from their mistakes, and the stupider ones don't. A little humor, too, always helps."

Eight: Eavesdropping on Enlightenment

"I do not disagree that the world is a complicated place," Miss Wollstonecraft allowed. "But I cannot see any right or humorous side to poverty or the subjugation of women."

"Perhaps the truth that matters most," Miss Austen smiled, looking out the restaurant's front window, "is that woman pinning a flower on her companion's shawl, or there, where that carriage driver is helping his passenger cross the sewage in the gutter. Perhaps the love and thoughtfulness you crave for yourself and for all the world most wholly exists in these small, often invisible, personal interchanges?"

Dot followed Miss Austen's gaze, but could not see what she was describing.

"I believe, Miss Austen," Miss Wordsworth observed, "that we must credit you, despite your youth, with having a thoughtful and perceptive mind of your own."

"Thank you, Miss Wordsworth. Yes, I do believe that one can do what is right from any station in life. Beating one's wings against the heaviest wind is not always necessary. Smaller victories also add up."

Miss Wollstonecraft looked as if she were about to disagree when Miss Wordsworth put on her gloves, saying, "Miss Wollstonecraft, Miss Austen, I must take my leave, as I feel my dental pain increasing. However, I believe we have some common conversational ground to hoe—perhaps our harvest may be of use to others. Plain living and high thinking describe the life my brother and Mr. Coleridge and I are building. Mr. Coleridge says we are three bodies with a single soul." Miss Wordsworth's voice softened as she mentioned Mr. Coleridge. "I hope I can persuade you to visit us in the Lake District."

As the three ladies rose to leave, gathering their parasols and adjusting their hats and shawls, Dot's mind was spinning with ideas and questions. She kept her eyes on the three ladies as they bustled out of the café. No one else looked their way. She remembered something her mother had said, a long time ago. "Travel isn't only going from place to place."

Nine: Sad and Mad

Next morning, Dot cracked open her eyes to see Aunt Tab on her knees in bed, hunched over like a parenthesis, peering out their small hotel window. Even barely awake, Dot could see over Aunt Tab's bony shoulder that the weather had turned against them. Rivulets of damp dirt coursed down the window pane; the sky was gray and low and spitting rain. The only bright spot in her field of vision was *Dancing on the Edge*, which she had hung over a lampshade as soon as they'd arrived. The boat with its sturdy masts and full sails was facing her.

Dot snuggled back down under Tinkerbell, who was now lying on top of her bed. Since Tink had been disembodied from her blue shag background, Dot thought she didn't belong on the floor anymore.

"It's only water," said Aunt Tab. "Places to go, things to do." She whipped Tink off Dot and pushed her out of her warm sheets and into their tiny bathroom and even tinier shower.

Dot stood groggily under a tepid trickle of water, groaning loudly and feeling abused. This pathetic English plumbing was a personal affront. At home, her mother had loved both hot showers and hot baths, and Dot felt the same way. It was their luxury. Thea once said, "Instead of movies and restaurants, we'll spend our money on hot water." And now this. Cold and wet, inside and out.

The day was not starting out well. Last night she'd had an odd dream about the three women in the soup café. She had no doubt that yesterday she'd seen what she'd seen and heard what she'd heard. In her dream, the women were back again, this time playing cards. But not regular cards

Nine: Sad and Mad

and she couldn't imagine how she'd invented them. They were larger than standard cards, and on each one was an elaborate colored drawing of swords or coins or sticks, with swirling clouds or stormy seas in the background. Some cards were flooded with bright yellow sunshine, others were gray and black. There were people on them, too; children dancing in fields of flowers and sad beggars in the snow and travelers on boats.

In her dream, the three women took turns laying out a few cards, pointing at them one by one, and then discussing something that Dot couldn't understand. A few times, they burst into loud laughter and looked over their shoulders.

It was one of those dreams that doesn't disappear when you wake up.

Dot quickly toweled off and dressed in her warmest sweatshirt. Her plan was to lie down on Tinkerbell and try to remember the dream in more detail. Maybe there was a message in it. Maybe it was about her mother. Maybe it was *from* her mother. She didn't know if that was possible. Likely not. But still.

She threw herself into her usual position on top of the pixie and stared at the white hotel sheets just past Tink's raggedy cut-out margins. The smooth pale sheets weren't as good an anchoring device as the blue yarn had been, but they would have to do.

Too soon, Aunt Tab emerged from her turn in the bathroom. "We'll need a good breakfast today to brave the elements," she said, as she pulled on an extra sweater. It took only one step of Aunt Tab's long legs to reach Dot's bed from the bathroom door. "Hey, none of that horizontal stuff. Get up, girl. It's already paid for—a Full English Breakfast."

Dot reluctantly rose and followed Aunt Tab downstairs. She was still thinking about the card game. She and Junie knew a few card tricks and her mother had taught her gin rummy and poker, but she'd never seen cards like these. The ladies were acting as if the cards were telling them a story. Maybe like fortune-telling? Once Thea had taken Dot to a circus and they'd had their fortunes told by an old woman dressed in layers of colorful skirts and a ruffled, embroidered blouse. It was all good news. So much for fortune-telling.

•••

If Aunt Tab had expected that Dot's mouth would water at the sight of Full English Breakfast, she was mistaken. Dot drifted by the counter display, hands in her jeans pockets, ignoring the warming trays and platters of food that no sensible person would consider to be breakfast food. Fried tomatoes. Pale, soupy-looking canned beans. Fried mushrooms. Steaming trays of fried eggs looked slightly more normal, but the bacon was limp and weird and right next to it was a pile of fried bread—not French toast, just naked, fried bread.

Next came something Dot heard another guest call blood sausage, which made Dot swallow hard. Luckily it wasn't red, but more of a blackish color, like an old scab. Gross. Next in line were bowls of canned peaches, canned grapefruit, wrinkly prunes, and fruit cocktail. Her mother would have had a fit over that last one. "Fruit cocktail is what they sweep up off the canning factory floor at the end of the day," her mother once told her.

Dot passed on all of the above and chose a box of very recognizable corn flakes.

"Try some," Aunt Tab said after they sat down, adding milk to a cup of mahogany dark tea and putting it in Dot's hands.

She did, and after the scalding part was over, she decided it wasn't too bad. Thea always had tea in the morning and again in the afternoon after Dot got home from school, but it had never occurred to Dot to try some herself. She picked at her corn flakes. Aunt Tab ate everything, and ended her feast by scooping beans over her toast.

"Terrific," Aunt Tab proclaimed. "Perfect start to your first day of Figuring Things Out."

"I'm going back to the room, Aunt Tab. You go figure things out; I don't feel good."

Nine: Sad and Mad

"Absolutely not, Dot. I didn't drag you halfway across the planet to commune with Tinkerbell."

"But, Aunt Tab—" Dot hated that she sounded like a baby, but felt completely unready to face the sidewalk again, two days in a row, marching around with Aunt Tab and her maps. It was so horribly, completely different from exploring Seattle with Thea.

"No buts, Miss Dorothy Mary-Jane. Today is for Mary Wollstonecraft. The only one of the three to be a mother. Not to mention a brilliant political firebrand. An eminently worthy namesake. Ten minutes. Don't forget to brush your teeth."

Dot divided her ten minutes into eight minutes on Tinkerbell and two minutes for teeth brushing and putting on her rain jacket. She remembered that Miss Wollstonecraft in the soup café was the talkative one with the dark curly hair and the run-on stories about jumping off a bridge even though she was a mother but being saved by fishermen, and guillotines in Paris and writing a book the other women both knew about.

When Aunt Tab came back to the room, Dot asked, "Did she have just one daughter?"

"Why do you ask that? No, as a matter of face, she had two. The second, also named Mary, became even more famous than her mother."

"Famous for what?"

"She wrote *Frankenstein*. When she was just nineteen."

Nineteen seemed old to Dot, but still on the kid side of being grown-up. When she'd turned twelve a few months ago, her mother said she could consider herself a teenager. Thea had always given Dot a choice of which day she wanted to celebrate her birthday on, because most people were busy with other things on December twenty-fifth. Some years she'd celebrated on June twenty-fifth, her half-birthday. This past year, she'd chosen December thirty-first, and had her party at midnight. Junie told her the city fireworks were just for her, and she was so happy she half-believed it. A typically wonderful **BT** memory. Suddenly realizing that her next birthday would be Thea-less, she started sniffling and started to fall onto Tinkerbell and her bed.

Aunt Tab was moving something from her suitcase to her small daypack, all the while keeping an eye on Dot.

"Off we go," she said in a staccato bark, grabbing Dot before she could make it to Tinkerbell. Handing her a hanky, she pushed Dot firmly ahead of her out the door and down the hall to the elevator. "Lift is what they call it here," Aunt Tab clicked her tongue, "even when it's going down it's called a lift."

Outside, the rain was still coming down, steady but not heavy; not so different from Seattle, Dot thought, and it perfectly matched her gray and chilly mood. The streets were crowded with taxis and buses, and the sidewalks were dotted with umbrellas, mostly black. Dot stayed close to the buildings, while Aunt Tab walked on the curb side, humming a few bars of *Singing in the Rain*.

"Where are we going?" Dot finally asked. "Not that I can do anything about it," she added, facing away from Aunt Tab so she wouldn't hear.

"Don't mutter, Dot. We're going to the River Thames to run a little errand for your mother."

"Aunt Tab, don't talk like that. It creeps me out."

"It's the truth. Can't quit now."

Dot's mood worsened. She didn't want to be outside, she didn't want to be so far from her yellow bedroom, and less and less did she want to be on this wild goose chase with Aunt Tab. As she tried to think of ways to get out of this pickle, she thought of the Piccadilly tube that they'd taken from Heathrow Airport. If she could steal her passport and plane ticket confirmation from Aunt Tab's daypack, she was sure she could figure out how to get back to the airport and change the day of her flight. She'd have to walk on some sidewalks by herself, but for something this important, she was sure she could make herself do it. Maybe she could even leave tonight. Back in her own room! Maybe Junie would sleep over for a night or two.

She sloshed along, hugging the stone sides of the buildings, eyeing Aunt Tab's daypack planted firmly on her bony shoulders. She wished she could fly—Tinkerbell never had to worry about airplanes or passports.

Nine: Sad and Mad

A large red truck rumbled by, causing her to entirely lose her forward progress. Escape was going to be harder than she thought, she admitted, as she huddled in the nearest doorway.

Aunt Tab didn't notice Dot had dropped behind until she was about a half-block ahead. She finally turned around and saw Dot cringing in the entrance to an office building.

"No giving up, Dot. We forge ahead," she said as she returned to where Dot had become rooted.

"I don't want to *be* here," she shouted, "I hate city streets." Even her Explosivision was failing her. Stupid, childish idea anyway.

"Maybe we can find a park to cut through," Aunt Tab said, pulling out her maps and dropping them in a puddle. She scooped them up and shook off the dirty water, pointing out big green patches among the crisscross of streets. "See this? Virginia Woolf said that you could walk London end-to-end entirely on green paths. Let's head over that way and follow her route."

Dot didn't know who Virginia Woolf was, but when she looked at the map, she realized it could work. Like hopping from one Ikea rug to another, you could walk across Hyde Park to Green Park to St. James Park and then you were practically at the squiggly blue River Thames.

"Wish you'd figured that out sooner," Dot grumped, not willing to sound grateful.

Another block and they stepped onto a park path. Dot's panic subsided. The big open green spaces were reassuring, with their tidy lines of huge chestnut trees leafing out in fragile spring green and only a few people walking around. Not a wheeled vehicle in sight.

The rain wasn't letting up, though. The grass was shimmery with water and the asphalt paths were turning into shallow creek beds. Dot and Aunt Tab's shoes were wet and water was osmosing up the legs of their pants. Their jacket hoods were up so they couldn't see around them very well and it was hard to talk. Not that Dot wanted to—with the panic damped down, weary sadness took over. She kept her head down, watching her wet feet alternating in front of her, right, left, right, left. She might as well be on a moving walkway going nowhere.

Splash, splash, nowhere, nowhere, never, never, neverland. Strangely, though, as much as she loved Tinkerbell, Peter Pan's Neverland had never appealed to her. It wasn't that it was too much about boys (she liked the fights with Captain Hook); it was that, in the end, even Wendy couldn't turn Neverland into a real home, a place where a real, growing life could happen.

Not that she had a chance for anything like that herself anymore. No matter how much her mother admired Dorothy Wordsworth, Mary Wollstonecraft, and Jane Austen, or how much *Dancing on the Edge* glowed with happy memories, Dot knew she was more of a small and weak Dot than she was a loyal, daring and inventive Dorothy Mary-Jane.

She kicked at a round pebble deposited by a miniature wave of rainwater on the park path. She kicked it along, right foot and then left foot, and each kick got larger and stronger. She looked for bigger rocks and hit them with increasing force. Her sad and lost feelings churned themselves into large and angry feelings. She was already mad at trucks and streets and libraries and clouds, but as she kicked her way along the path, her anger grew to include cities and countries, the whole planet, all of time—past, present, and future, and even the entire universe. And, she realized quite clearly, she was especially furious at Aunt Tab, the bossy interloper who was wrecking her life.

She returned to her plan to snag her passport and ticket information from Aunt Tab's daypack.

Ten: Connecting the Dots

"Here's the bridge," said Aunt Tab. They'd left the park and were now stopped stock still on a wide sidewalk that continued over a blue-painted steel and concrete bridge. Bus and car traffic thundered across it in both directions, spraying greasy water on their already soaked feet.

"Westminster Bridge dead ahead. Not the same one as Mary jumped from, but it'll do. Same river. Pick a side."

Dot, suddenly paying attention, looked up at Aunt Tab but didn't answer beyond a muttered, "Getting creepy again."

"Let's take the south side. More dramatic. And the wind's right."

Dot slowly followed Aunt Tab onto the bridge, afraid and fascinated at the same time. She felt like a moth who can't *not* flutter near the light, even after she has watched her buddies burn to a crisp.

The rain beat steadily on the concrete and steel. As they went farther out on the bridge, the churning surface of the river grew louder in Dot's ears. Aunt Tab stopped in the middle of the bridge and faced the water. Dot stood a few feet away, carefully out of reach of her aunt's long arms. Aunt Tab's spookiness was scary, but now she seemed to have forgotten Dot's existence. Keeping her eyes on the water, Aunt Tab swung her daypack off her shoulders.

Dot watched, mesmerized, as Aunt Tab pulled a small glass jelly jar out of the bottom of her pack. It was wrapped in tinfoil. She slowly unwrapped it.

"Thea, Thea," she whispered, holding the glass jar over the painted iron railing. "Here you go, but you will never be gone."

Ten: Connecting the Dots

Dot stared at Aunt Tab's hands, wet and pale in the rain, holding the jelly jar. With the tinfoil wrapping gone, she could see a small pile of gray sandy stuff inside the glass.

"Aunt Tab—"

"Yes, Dot? Want to unscrew the lid?"

"What is that?" Dot's voice came out in a squeak.

"Some of Thea. Her ashes. We're going to put them in the river."

Dot didn't know if this was creepier than what she had been thinking or not. Whatever it was, she was freaked, unable to speak, unwilling to move closer to her aunt.

Aunt Tab looked at Dot for a moment and then said, "Never mind, I'll do it this time." She unscrewed the lid and then, extending her long arm over the side, she turned the jar upside down. The delicate cascade of sandy ash flowed almost straight down and then dispersed lightly across the choppy water of the River Thames. It hung suspended like a lace handkerchief for a few seconds, then slipped, still holding together, below the surface.

Neither Dot nor Aunt Tab moved their eyes off the water for a very long time. It was as if they, too, were suspended and wet, as indeed they were, in the rain on the bridge.

• • •

They sloshed back to their hotel, Aunt Tab staying quiet and Dot stomping puddles. Her fury at Aunt Tab had returned and multiplied. How could she have pulled a trick like that?

"I'd wanted to visit Mary Wollstonecraft's grave," was all Aunt Tab said when they arrived at their hotel. "But we can't because it's been moved out of town. Her daughter Mary used to visit the cemetery a lot when it was here; it's where she and the poet Shelley fell in love. Right on her mother's grave. She wasn't much older than you."

Dot ignored her. She wasn't about to ask any questions, no matter how curious Aunt Tab made her about Mary Wollstonecraft's daughter

Mary who wrote *Frankenstein* when she was still a teenager and now apparently had fallen in love on her mother's grave. And with the poet Shelley, too. It was hard to keep quiet, now that he was in the story, because Shelley was one of her mother's favorite poets. Along with Coleridge and Wordsworth, who were in this story too, at least according to Miss Wordsworth from the soup café. And how did Mary Wollstonecraft die, anyway?

As Dot pointedly turned away from Aunt Tab, she saw a sign pasted on a clunky square computer in a corner of the lobby announcing "Internet Use for Hotel Guests Only."

"I'm going to send an email to Junie."

"Okay. I'll go up and get into some dry clothes," Aunt Tab said, sounding discouraged. Dot had never heard Aunt Tab sound discouraged before.

Dot surfed around the internet for a while, looking up plane schedules between London and Seattle (several a day) and the weather in Seattle (scattered showers). She looked at her house on Google Earth and wished it were a webcam so she could know for sure it was still there. She thought about looking up Dorothy Wordsworth, Mary Wollstonecraft, and Jane Austen on Wikipedia, but didn't. Her mother had once told her that Wikipedia had its place, but Direct Research, if possible, was always better. *Be Daring*.

Staring past the screen, past the dowdy hotel lobby, out into the damp London street, Dot had an inkling that Direct Research was indeed possible. In fact, she thought, maybe she should run away from Aunt Tab but *not* go home. Maybe she should stay in England instead. Check out these ladies on her own. Find out why her mom was so attached to them. She'd need money to do that—pounds, she remembered they were called. That made it more difficult—but not necessarily impossible. *Be Inventive*.

She switched to her Hotmail account. She had a message from Junie.

```
Hiya Dot, Did you see the northern lights?
Did they look like dancing shaggy icicles?
```

55

Ten: Connecting the Dots

> Mr. Cyrus says hi. What's England like? Is your Aunt Tab dragging you around places? ttyl Junie

Dot replied.

> Junie, Maybe there were northern lights, but we were too far from a window to see… those planes are big and nasty kids ride them.
>
> London is big too, bigger than Seattle and way too much traffic. The buses are **RED**—this is not a good trip! I think my spooky Aunt Tab wants to drop my mom's ashes all over this country. Today she dropped some into the Thames River, but they say it backwards…River Thames, pronounced Tems. It was pouring down rain. I freaked when I saw the ash—it's more like tiny gravelly sand than ash. I couldn't stop looking at it. It totally weirded me out.
>
> There's also something strange going on with three old fashioned ladies who are famous. And dead. For like 200 years. But I saw them. I heard them. They drank a lot of tea. Do you believe in time travel? Did I ever tell you what my whole name is? It's Dorothy Mary-Jane. Three names—three

ladies. Are you starting to get it? Am I going crazy?

I might come home early—Aunt Tab is bugging me. Or maybe I'll stay in England forever. My mom must have thought it was a pretty important place. Wish she'd told me more.

Write back!
Ta-ta —that means bye here.
Dot, alias DOROTHY MARY-JANE

PS: did you know that Frankenstein was written by a 19 year old girl? She ran away with Shelley, one of my Mom's favorite poets. The Frankenstein Mary was the daughter of the Mary that my mom named me after. I don't know too much about that Mary—she was some kind of revolutionary who tried to kill herself. See why I'm weirded out?

Eleven: Frankenstein's Mother

Next morning, Dot made Aunt Tab stop at a bookstore so she could buy a copy of *Frankenstein*. Other than that she wasn't talking. She was punishing Aunt Tab for pulling her mother's ashes out of her bag like that without any warning, and for this whole stupid trip in the first place. So far, she hadn't learned anything useful about her names or found any reason that would make living in the AT world worth the trouble. In fact, the world seemed to be a worse place than it was a week ago, before she'd come to England, and that was a direction that she hadn't thought possible.

"Miss Jane Austen is next," said Aunt Tab as they left the bookstore. "Good-bye, London. Hello, Alton. That's a little town in Hampshire county south of London." She flipped open a guidebook and pointed at Miss Austen's hometown, a small dot with a few spidery roads running through it.

Jane Austen was the youngest of the three at the soup café, Dot remembered (even though she was trying to ignore Aunt Tab); the one who kept pouring the tea and looking around. She seemed to be the best noticer of the women. Junie was like that—she was always noticing things like birds in trees or the good candy in the sale bin. Junie was the one who always noticed if other kids were really upset at school, even if they were perfectly quiet about it. Dot wondered if that was a skill you could learn, or if you were just born with it.

God knows what we'll do in Alton, Dot thought. Knowing Aunt Tab, something unexpected, but at least now she felt more prepared. She'd hoped that last night she'd get back into her dream of the three ladies

Eleven: Frankenstein's Mother

playing with that strange deck of cards, but it hadn't happened. The only other thing she remembered was something the dream Miss Austen had said about how the cards were like the parts of a story and when you put them all together in the right way it was like they came alive. That reminded Dot of *Dancing on the Edge*, and how her mom turned small silk squares into pictures that made you think and dream. Better than fortune-tellling.

• • •

They packed their suitcases and took the Tube to Waterloo train station, where Aunt Tab bought two tickets to Alton. The ticket seller smiled and said, "Ah, two Janeites, I see." Aunt Tab seemed to know what she was referring to, and replied, "My niece here is named after Miss Austen."

"Lovely. It's about an hour's ride. The train leaves on Track 6 in fifteen minutes."

"So civilized!" Aunt Tab sighed, as she stopped to buy two cups of tea at a stand on the way to Track 6.

The train was there, painted sky-blue with rows of doors along both sides of each car. The doors opened onto sets of facing seats, so passengers could get on and off directly from where they sat. Dot was surprised at how quickly Aunt Tab mastered the door latch. That sort of mechanical thing often had flummoxed her mother. Thea even had trouble with vacuum cleaner attachments.

"Look at this, Dot," Aunt Tab said, opening the window nearest their seat after they'd arranged their suitcases on the floor around their feet. "English engineers trust the average train-rider to figure out how to open and close doors and windows without hurting themselves. Never happen in America. See how traveling teaches you about where you're from, as much as where you've gone to?"

Dot had to admit that Aunt Tab was trying to be nice, so as she took her tea, she relented enough to say thanks. Dot was liking tea more and more. It had a definite soothing quality—maybe it was the warmth and the milk. Not soothing enough to jettison her plans to run away, though;

really, it did just the opposite. Drinking tea made her feel grown-up and capable.

Slurping expertly, Dot turned to look outside as the train slid away from the city. The scenery was not at all like the dark, pointy fir trees and sharp, snowy mountain faces she was used to seeing outside Seattle. This English landscape was lumpy and pale. The broad leafy trees were like open vases and the grassy fields had a buttery sheen to them. She wouldn't have been surprised to see a Hobbit village, round doorways and all. She wondered if she could live in a place like this. Maybe in a little country hamlet, like that one off in the distance—it didn't look as if much truck traffic at all went through it.

Aunt Tab interrupted Dot's planning. "We're deep into Jane Austen's home territory now. She never traveled much at all, only around this southern part of England and only in the company of her family. Very different from Mary Wollstonecraft, who took off by herself in sailing boats to Portugal and Norway and went to Paris during the French Revolution."

"Mom and I rented a movie about Jane Austen."

"Not surprised. Miss Austen is the one of your three who's most popular nowadays. Wasn't always true."

Dot didn't want to give Aunt Tab the sense that they were entirely on friendly terms, so she just gave a curt nod. In fact, she didn't remember much of anything about Jane Austen, just that her mother had loved the movie and that the women all wore long dresses, like in the soup café, and that the long shots of the scenery looked exactly like what they were passing through right now.

Aunt Tab tried a different tack. "We'll be staying at a bed-and-breakfast. It's someone's home and they rent out a spare room. You need to be polite."

Dot snipped, "Don't worry, I know how."

"Thought maybe you'd forgotten."

Dot answered by opening her copy of *Frankenstein*. It was a slim paperback with a black-and-white drawing of a lopsided giant with crazed eyes staggering across a snowy field with a small hut and gnarled, leafless

61

Eleven: Frankenstein's Mother

trees in the background. Right away in the first pages, Victor Frankenstein's mother dies, and he describes his shock and sadness:

It is so long before the mind can persuade itself that she whom we saw every day and whose very existence appeared a part of our own can have departed forever—that the brightness of a beloved eye can have been extinguished and the sound of a voice so familiar and dear to the ear can be hushed, never more to be heard. These are the reflections of the first days; but when the lapse of time proves the reality of the evil, then the actual bitterness of grief commences.

Got it in one, thought Dot. This Mary Wollstonecraft Shelley knew what she was writing about—it just doesn't seem possible that a person can disappear so completely, to be so alive and present, and then be so utterly gone and absent forever. Dot wondered again how and when Mary Wollstonecraft had died.

She kept reading until the train stopped at the Alton station.

Twelve: A Good Laugh

No. 4 Hanger's Close was the address of the Alton bed-and-breakfast that Aunt Tab had found on the internet. It was one in a row of six connected brick houses not far from the train station. The whole street looked neglected, but not in a scary or romantic way, just in a tired way, like keeping up with the repairs was no longer anyone's top priority. Each house in the row had a front yard the size of a beach towel, separated from the sidewalk by a low, continuous brick and stone wall. Most of the yards were decorated with nothing more than broken concrete and weeds.

Except for No. 4. Its brick was spiffy and clean and neatly mortared. Dot noted approvingly that the bricks were an unthreatening mottled-brown color, not red at all. No. 4's tiny yard was bursting with spring bulbs and silly plastic whirligigs. Window boxes spilled white petunias down the brick front, and a gaggle of plaster garden gnomes welcomed visitors from the front gate. Dot and Aunt Tab crossed the yard in three short steps, bumping their suitcases across stepping stones shaped like lily pads to reach the closet-sized front porch. Aunt Tab knocked sharply on the heavy wood door, which opened almost immediately.

"Come in, come in! You must be my new American friends! Delighted!"

Dot and Aunt Tab were practically sucked into the house by the woman's cheerful welcome, as she windmilled her arms around and dragged them inside. Dot hovered behind Aunt Tab to avoid being hugged.

Aunt Tab finally managed to squeeze out a harrumphing hello, and admitted that indeed they were the Americans who had rented the room for

Twelve: A Good Laugh

the next two days. Dot enjoyed seeing her aunt outdone by someone else's cascade of conversation.

"I'm Mrs. Whitley, and I'm *so* pleased to meet you. It's so *wonderful* of you to have come all this way to our little Alton." Mrs. Whitley brushed flour off a huge flowered apron that barely made it around her plump middle. When she noticed the cloud of white she'd stirred up, she said, "Oh my goodness me, the scones! I can't have them burning, now can I? Your room's off to the right, down there and the lav is on the left," she added, pointing with a floury finger as she bounced off in the other direction.

"She means the bathroom," Aunt Tab said as they rolled their suitcases down the hall. "Although it might be just a sink and not the toilet, which might be in a room called the WC, which means Water Closet—"

"Okay, Aunt Tab. I get it. You studied this stuff." Dot was irritated. She was starting to feel proprietary about England, and it didn't fit into her plan that Aunt Tab knew more about the place than she did. She pushed ahead and opened the door to their room, where she was immediately engulfed in a pink and blue mass of flowered everything—the bed, the walls, the lampshades, the curtains, the rug, every single surface was covered in great swaths of pastel-flowered fabric. There were flounces and ruffles and swooping fabric everywhere, all in pastel colors that somehow managed to clash terribly with each other.

"Dreadful," Aunt Tab said, coming up behind Dot and shaking her head. "Not Thea's colors, that's for sure!" Then she started to laugh, and barky though it was, her laugh was infectious, because Dot could exactly see her point. Her mother *would* think it hilarious that Dot was swathed in pastel as she plumbed the mysteries of Miss Jane Austen. A wave of laughter snuck up on Dot, the first in ages, and she couldn't stop it. It didn't take long for both Dot and Aunt Tab to be laughing so hard they had to let go of their suitcases and sit down on the bed.

"Be polite, now," Dot said to Aunt Tab in her most grown-up voice, as they finally pulled themselves together.

"Exactly what Miss Austen would say. Best behavior, I promise. But how about I drape your *Dancing on the Edge* across that curtain rod real quick?"

Dot unpacked Tinkerbell and *Dancing on the Edge*. Shaking Tink around the room to boldly fight off toxic clouds of pink and blue, she handed the silk collage to Aunt Tab to hang up. She knew her mother would still be laughing.

While discovering the idiosyncrasies of the toilet, (the flush lever was a rope hanging from a tank on the wall high above the toilet bowl), Dot heard Mrs. Whitley singing in the kitchen. Thea had sung in the kitchen, too, lovely tunes that matched the sweets that came out of her oven. Thea loved baking desserts. Hearing the singing in the kitchen, Dot suddenly had a taste for her mother's favorite—gingerbread. Thea's gingerbread was unbeatably dark and dense, with exactly the right amount of gingery sharpness. Just another one of those perfect things from **BT** that she'd never have again.

She couldn't believe she'd been laughing just a few minutes ago.

Leaving the bathroom, Dot followed the sounds of eating and drinking down the hall. She found Aunt Tab and Mrs. Whitley in the living room, pouring tea and eating hot scones with blackberry jam. Between bites and slurps, Aunt Tab unfolded maps while Mrs. Whitley handed her piles of tourist brochures about Alton and its famous resident, Miss Jane Austen.

"Yes, thank you Mrs. Whitley, but now Dot and I will stretch our legs around town and find ourselves some dinner," Aunt Tab said, her mouth still full of scone crumbs.

"That's the best thing about English tea. You've hit it spot on," Mrs. Whitley laughed all the way through her thick body. "Here, young Dot, have some tea and scones." Mrs. Whitley plumped a blue-flowered pillow for Dot and handed her a tea cup and a scone smeared with jam and what looked like whipped sour cream on a small, green, leaf-shaped plate. "You can have a delicious tea and almost immediately afterwards eat a lovely dinner as well."

Twelve: A Good Laugh

Dot sat down and sipped the tea and tasted the scone. It was not as good as gingerbread, but not completely inedible either. It had crunchy sugar crystals all over the top. She sat there, listening to Mrs. Whitley's laughter. A lot of laughing seemed to go on in this house—the most she'd heard so far in this **AT** world.

As Mrs. Whitley waved them out the door with her dish towel, Aunt Tab and Dot stepped carefully between the gnomes and the whirligigs, and turned left toward Alton's town center. Dot noticed that people still drove on the wrong side of the street, same as in London. The sidewalks here were wider than in London though, and made of big stone slabs. There weren't many cars on the road, either, and the road was separated from the sidewalk by strong protective-looking curbs made of heavy pieces of rectangular granite. The curbs were high, too, making it hard for a vehicle to jump onto the sidewalk and sideswipe a pedestrian. All in all, Dot approved of the safety features in Jane Austen's territory. Even so, she kept well to the inside of the sidewalk, in her accustomed track far from the curb.

It was late afternoon, and the dipping sun was throwing trails of waning light across the warm stone and brick walls. She and Aunt Tab shared the sidewalk with people carrying groceries, or a newspaper, or bunches of fragrant spring peonies. On one block, a swarm of teenage boys in shorts and striped jerseys, all legs and giant feet, leapt around them, pushing each other, taking up the entire sidewalk, reliving their afternoon soccer match. At home, Aunt Tab would have yelled at them, but here, she didn't; merely saying, "I remember once watching you play soccer when you were little. They call it football here."

Dot didn't say anything. Actually, she'd never much liked soccer except for the running around part. And these soccer boys reminded her that the only other English kids she'd seen had been those nasty twins on the plane. At least, the boy had been nasty.

Aunt Tab then slipped into tour guide mode and Dot slipped into not-listening mode, although she couldn't help but gather that Alton was a small and very old town with not much industry, and that the main reason anybody visited was because of the Jane Austen connection. Dot and Aunt Tab explored several streets, some residential like Hanger's Close, and some with small stores selling clothing or shoes or small appliances. They stopped at a plaza near the center of town. In the middle of the open space, there was a stone tower with names carved in a spiral from top to bottom.

"It's an obelisk, Dot. Now there's a good word for you."

"I know, Aunt Tab. We already had Egyptian history."

"Well, anyway, this one is commemorating the local men who died in World War I. Have you had that in history already?"

"Of course," Dot said, although she hadn't. She'd heard about World War II, so she supposed there must have been a World War I, but she couldn't remember anything about it. Maybe it had happened here? She wondered if Jane Austen had been killed in World War I, but she wasn't going to ask.

As she looked at the names, she remembered again Mary Wollstonecraft's talk about the American and the French revolutions. She thought again about Mr. Cyrus' history class. The Americans and the English had been enemies during the American Revolution, but now they're best friends. How do changes like that happen? History is slippery stuff, she thought. In more ways than one.

Aunt Tab interrupted her philosophical thinking with some loud sniffing. Folding her map, she said, "Ah, hot oil…fish and chips. This way!"

A short walk bought them to a stridently yellow and blue fish and chips shop, manned by a single lounging teenager with pale, dirty hair, and watery, unfocused eyes. Even though the door set off a tinkling bell when they walked in, he didn't look up from reading the sports section of the paper.

"Young man, where's your customer service?" Aunt Tab said after they had waited quietly for at least a full minute.

"Whatcha want?" the boy said, pointing to the menu on a chalkboard dangling above the counter.

What is it about English boys, Dot thought, that they are all so rude and unbearable? No wonder Mary Wollstonecraft wrote about

Twelve: A Good Laugh

women's rights. That reminded Dot that she wanted to read more *Frankenstein*. It was getting interesting. And scary.

The fish and chip choices on the chalkboard turned out to be complicated and full of local vernacular that neither Dot nor Aunt Tab understood. They finally resorted to picking one of the more generic-looking items, and came out of the shop holding two very hot bags of deep-fried cod and lots of fries, liberally sprinkled with salt and vinegar. The oily scent from the store trailed after them and clung to their clothes.

"Mrs. Whitley better have a washing machine we can use," said Aunt Tab as she licked salt off her fingers.

"Internet, too," added Dot, who wanted to see what Junie had to say about her plans to run away. Maybe she'd have some thoughts about the choice of coming home or staying in England. Probably too much to hope she could come here.

The bags kept their food incredibly hot while they wandered down the street and found a bench to sit on in a small park a few blocks away. The bench seat was still warm from the sun.

"Of course, there were no cars or buses in Miss Austen's day, but the town streets were the same. She probably stood in this exact spot, talking to her sister, looking across this same park, seeing those hills beyond, enjoying a sunset just like this one." Aunt Tab was certainly in an expansive mood.

Dot was surprised that she liked her fish and chips. She was actually enjoying sitting outside, tearing off chunks of fish with her fingers and getting a drippy bite of fish and salt and fried potato all at the same time. The little breezes and chirping birds in the tree branches helped, too.

"You realize, Dot, that the air we are breathing this very second is chock-full of molecules that Miss Austen herself once breathed into her body and then exhaled."

"Don't talk like that!" Dot choked. Aunt Tab sounded like Victor Frankenstein discovering how to breathe life into his stitched-together Monster.

"Like what? It's perfectly true. Miss Austen once said that 'imagination is everything' but I don't happen to agree with that. Imagination is important, but so is knowledge. Not to mention wisdom, which you are too young to even think about yet."

"Am not," Dot said automatically, and then added, thinking of what she'd read in the preface to *Frankenstein* about how Mary had run away from home with her true love Shelley just a month short of her seventeenth birthday. "I'm not too young for anything. I could run away if I wanted to."

"I certainly hope not. Thea would never forgive me."

"You creep me out, Aunt Tab," Dot said, sucking salt off her fingers and worrying that she shouldn't have mentioned running away. Even though she'd had a friendly laugh with Aunt Tab back at Mrs. Whitley's, and even though she seemed to be enjoying food for the first time AT, she was no less resolved to run away. If anything, the scales were tipping in favor of staying in England.

Aunt Tab seemed not to have heard. "Tomorrow is for Jane Austen. After we see her house, we'll have lunch at Cassandra's Cup. Mrs. Whitley says it's a little tea shop right across the road from the Austen house."

Thirteen: Lost

Dot didn't sleep well that night because Aunt Tab kept flapping her arms around on the bed, taking up way more than her half. Her legs jiggled, too. She hoped the next place they stayed had two beds again. She finally got up and pulled *Dancing on the Edge* around her shoulders, sat in the chair and read *Frankenstein* using the pale light from a streetlamp outside. She eventually fell asleep sideways, partly on the chair and partly on the floor. She dreamed of the book's mountainous countryside and imagined she was Victor Frankenstein's beloved sister Elizabeth, walking in the rain and lightning, worrying about why her brother was so haunted and unhappy.

Only Elizabeth wasn't really Victor Frankenstein's sister, although they'd been raised together. She was actually the daughter of a poor shepherd's family and had been adopted by Victor's parents. Victor and Elizabeth loved each other and planned to marry someday, and this was okay with everyone.

Dot woke up thinking about taking walks in the woods, preferably minus the rain and the lightning. Maybe that's what she should do; take a walk that would be a practice runaway, to see what really running away would be like. She had to decide about her choices—run away to stay in England or run away to take an earlier flight home. If she decided to stay in England, she needed to choose between the countryside, like Alton, or London, the big city. She was starting to like the idea of staying, but it would definitely require more planning.

"I'm going to take a walk by myself," Dot announced to Aunt Tab in Mrs. Whitley's sunny breakfast room, where their flowered tablecloth

Thirteen: Lost

was almost invisible under the ingredients for a Full English Breakfast. "I'll meet you in front of Cassandra's Cup."

"Excellent thought. To live is to grow. I'll give you a map." Aunt Tab was deep in smearing warm egg yolk on a piece of toast with one hand and pouring cream into a teacup with the other. "Here, have some."

Dot accepted the food quietly even though she wasn't hungry. She didn't want to wake Aunt Tab up because she certainly must still be asleep to have agreed so easily to Dot's walk.

The map Aunt Tab gave Dot after breakfast was no rough sketch of the area. It was called an Ordnance Survey Map, and as Dot unfolded it, she saw it had little houses and buildings drawn all over it, locating everything from phone booths to castles. Churches were drawn with tiny spires, towers, minarets, or domes according to their ecclesiastical bent. Tiny vegetation icons showed whether the greenery was coniferous, non-coniferous, orchard, scrub, bracken, heath, or reedy marsh land.

"Jeez, Aunt Tab, where did you find this? Terrorists would love this."

"No slang, young lady, and I don't know what you mean. The English are wonderful walkers—"

"They have to be, with all the eating they do."

"—and they've mapped out their whole country like this. You'll probably come across all sorts of people on your walk. Here's a path that goes to our lunch place." Aunt Tab drew her skinny finger along a dashed line that wound its way through some woods and over a stream, ending right near the Cassandra's Cup tea shop. "The Austen house, here, is right across the road from Cassandra's Cup. Jane's big sister was named Cassandra," Aunt Tab said, sounding as if big sisters always deserved the credit for whatever a little sister might produce.

"Cassandra was a beautiful woman in Greek mythology who always told the truth but nobody believed her." Aunt Tab harrumphed into her tea cup.

"Right," said Dot, not paying attention as she folded up the map and went back to their room to get ready. She shoved *Frankenstein* and a pencil into her daypack and pulled on her sweatshirt. She brushed her hand against *Dancing on the Edge,* a habit she'd gotten into this week. It was strengthening somehow, to feel the silk her mother had sewn, and the words that her mother had embroidered. She looked at her hands. Maybe Aunt Tab's molecule talk hadn't been so weird after all—maybe some molecules from her mother's hands were now on her hands.

Be Daring
Be Inventive
Be Loyal

As she was rubbing a silken edge on her cheek, she realized that this moment might be her best chance to find her passport and plane information in Aunt Tab's bag. Aunt Tab would be occupied with her Full English Breakfast a little while longer. Maybe Mrs. Whitley would even appear and start jabbering.

Dot carefully shut the door to their room and quickly opened Aunt Tab's conveniently unzipped and messy suitcase. It was easy to dig around—no worries about disturbing anything because everything was already plenty disturbed. The only thing she was worried about, besides Aunt Tab barging in, was bumping up against a jar of ash. She didn't want that to happen. She wasn't ready for that yet. If she ever would be.

She found the two passports in a side pocket along with Aunt Tab's underwear. "Yuck," said Dot out loud as she felt the cotton and elastic and realized what she was feeling. She hoped at least it was clean. Even so, she wiped her passport with the corner of a bed sheet before she stowed it safely in her back jeans pocket. Then she felt around a little more for the papers with the airplane confirmation numbers. No dice. That might present a problem; she'd have to think about that some more. Maybe Junie'd have some ideas. That was the other thing—after lunch she'd ask if she could use Mrs. Whitley's computer.

Thirteen: Lost

First things first, though. She patted down Aunt Tab's suitcase mess, picked up her jacket and daypack, and walked back to the breakfast room, very conscious of the stiff paper rectangle in her back pocket.

"See you at lunch, Aunt Tab. Thanks for the map." Very casual.

"Noon sharp. Take my watch." Aunt Tab took off her battered Timex and gave it Dot, who put it in her front jeans pocket and walked out the door.

It was the first time she'd walked outside by herself since **BT**, and it made her feel both brave and doomed. The only reason she could even consider doing it was because she didn't have to cross any streets to get to the start of the path. Even so, she wouldn't have been surprised if something evil and predatory swooped down on her—a giant red vulture or a helicopter gunship or Victor Frankenstein's Monster. She glanced up at the clear blue and empty sky. A few finches twittered from bushes outside Mrs. Whitley's front door. Despite this friendly welcome she walked carefully along the inner edge of the Hanger's Close sidewalk until she found the beginning of the path, which veered off between two low houses, like an alley, but green.

When she got away from the houses and streets, and felt more able to look around calmly, she found herself on a path that edged a neatly farmed countryside, placid and organic. She was nowhere near a paved road and couldn't hear a single traffic sound. As she settled into the walk, she thought *I can do this*. She felt comfortable, almost as good as the old **BT** days when she was a kid who was loved in a world that was good. It was even better than lying on Tinkerbell.

The landscape was so peaceful and colorful. She imagined she was an explorer inside a rotating kaleidoscope. She tramped around, watching the colored shapes slip into elegant new patterns, blues and greens shimmering back and forth, punctuated with deep golds and oranges. Miss Jane Austen sure had lived in a beautiful country.

About thirty minutes out of town, she passed a farmer in dirty, green rubber boots, heavy canvas pants and a gray-checked corduroy shirt. He was tending a burning pile of leaves and old stumps. At first the fire looked natural and normal out there in the field, another part of the kaleidoscope, kicking up warm yellows and oranges. But then **AT** life caught up with her and the fire's snaps and sparks shouted loss and death, and the sight of ashes gave her the shakes. She stumbled away from the flames, a thin film of tears obscuring her path with a wavy uncertainty.

When she'd recovered a little, she thought about the countryside that *Frankenstein*'s Monster was walking through in Mary's book. It was very different from this, packed with snowy mountains and drenching rain and lots of thunder and lightning. At first, the Monster had stomped around, not knowing anything—he didn't know any language, he didn't know about night and day, he didn't know about food or sleep, he didn't know anything about how his body worked. All he knew was that when people saw him, they screamed and ran away or attacked him. One person shot him in the shoulder. That was before he'd killed anyone himself.

She rubbed her own shoulder for a minute, feeling sorry for the Monster. After all, it had no mother at all. At least I had a mother for twelve years. Dot smiled a tentative smile when she thought that.

As she walked on, Dot noticed that her path was taking her out of the fields and into a forested valley. At the edge of the valley, the path zigzagged down a sharp series of switchbacks and then straightened out at the bottom, near a small creek visible in patches through trees along its banks.

She started down, concentrating carefully on her steps because the switchbacks were short, steep, and slippery. From what she remembered about the Jane Austen movie she'd watched with Thea, women in those days didn't have very good shoes for this sort of thing. Even her own sneakers didn't have much traction, and she slipped a couple times, once landing on her butt.

"Shit," she said as she felt the cool damp soak through her jeans. Worried about her passport, she fished it out and zipped it deep inside her daypack. Although Dot was completely unrepentant about swearing, she suspected Miss Jane Austen would have used more inventive words to indicate her distress.

Thirteen: Lost

When she reached the river at the bottom of the valley, her path divided like a "T," one branch going one way down the river and the other branch following the river in the opposite direction. Which direction went to Cassandra's Cup? Dot had no idea.

She dug out the Ordnance Survey map, but it was no help because she couldn't figure out where she was. "To get to where you want to go, you need to know where you are," Thea had said once when they were deciphering a bus schedule for one of their summer visits to Seattle's industrial flats. Seemed as if the advice applied just as much to walking in the woods.

Dot stood still at the intersecting top of the path's "T." She looked first one way and then the other. Both looked identical—fairly straight and then turning about a hundred yards on, following two bends in the creek, one to the right and one to the left. Leafy trees on both sides obscured most of the sunlight. No signs, no clues about which way might lead to Cassandra's Cup.

The shade brought a chill to the valley, and both paths were muddy. The wet spot on Dot's jeans was cold, and her toes were damp and chilly. None of this helped. She wasn't sure how to make it better.

She found an almost-dry rock just off the path, near the creek, and sat down. In the surround-sound of the woods, she heard the stream swooshing and eddying over its rocky bottom. Birds, hidden amongst tree branches, called peremptorily to each other. Not knowing what else to do, waiting for an idea, she took *Frankenstein* out of her pack and started to read. She had almost finished it last night.

The Monster was on a murderous rampage. He'd already killed Victor's little brother and Victor's best friend. Dot could tell that his adopted sister and fiancée Elizabeth was next. The Monster could see that Victor and Elizabeth were happy together, and so he asked Victor to make him a girlfriend, too. Dot thought it was a perfectly reasonable request, and at first Victor agreed. Then he changed his mind and it was that refusal that set the Monster off on his murder spree. The only saving feature from Dot's perspective was that all the deaths in the story were completely bloodless. Suffocation or some such relatively clean method. No red at all.

Dot read on, the pages almost turning themselves, until it was over. Almost everyone died. The Monster was an incredibly scary and unfortunate piece of work. At the end he went off to commit suicide on the Arctic tundra. It was one of those "no good will come of this" kind of stories. Unhappy and a little spooked, Dot was sad to imagine the nineteen-year-old author Mary being so pessimistic, but she could easily empathize. Sometimes life just went that way.

Dot closed *Frankenstein* and remembered she was lost. She stood up and again peered down the two directions of the "T" in the path. This time, she noticed a small cottage through the trees near the bend on the left side of the "T." Stowing her book away, she picked up her pack and walked toward it, thinking maybe she could ask directions.

It was a small stone house, modernized with sliding glass doors and a blue tile roof. A child's yellow plastic slide stood in a corner of the small grassy yard and a homemade swing hung from a nearby tree. A square vegetable garden had been dug and strings were stretched across it, marking the rows where a few seedlings had appeared.

Dot remembered an early part in *Frankenstein* when the Monster stumbled on an isolated Swiss hut and spied on its inhabitants for months. Hiding, he watched Felix and Agatha care for their blind father as they scratched a poor living from the hard earth. Gradually, the Monster learned their language, but more importantly, he learned about families and kindness and love. Mary's writing showed how badly the Monster wanted to be a part of them, how much he wanted a family of his own.

The Monster gathered wood and secretly left it on the little family's doorstep and weeded their garden in the middle of the night. Eventually, he got up the courage to show himself to them, still fearful from his past experience of being attacked, but now that he could talk, he hoped to be able to explain himself. He hoped they would be nice to him.

But they weren't. Felix and Agatha, and even the blind father, screamed and tried to beat him, and that's when the Monster became hateful and vengeful and murderous.

"Such an out-of-the-way spot, isn't this?"

Dot almost jumped out of her skin. She turned around to face her fate.

But no, the being that had crept up on her unnoticed was no Monster, but was a young woman in a long, blue-striped dress, a shawl, a bonnet and thin shoes.

"Um, yes," said Dot, coughing to cover up her almost-scream.

"Such a pleasant day for a walk, don't you agree? I haven't seen you around my village before, have I?"

"Um, no, I'm visiting," Dot said, stumbling on her words.

"How delightful. Where are you from, if I may ask?"

"Seattle. It's in America," she added, when the young woman looked puzzled.

"My goodness, you *are* a traveler. I have been no farther than London. Isn't Hampshire the loveliest county in England? Our trees are so elegant and the water so clear." The stranger nodded her head to indicate the beauties around them. "And what brings you to my neighborhood, if I may inquire?"

Dot was as stuck for an answer as she had been on the plane when that awful boy, Nick, had asked her the same question.

"Well, my mother died, and..." Dot stopped and looked down at her wet sneakers, concentrating hard on the complicated backward pattern of the laces that Junie had strung for her ages ago, trying with all her might to turn off the memory reel showing the puddles of red around her mother's head.

"Oh, you poor dear! How unfortunate indeed," the woman said when it became clear that Dot wasn't going to say anything more. "Thank the dear Lord, my own mother, a most loving and joyful woman, is well at the moment, although health is always so uncertain. But do not despair, my new friend. I am very interested in girls who have no mothers, or else very useless ones, and in my experience their lives always come out quite well. Indeed, in all the stories I invent, there is not a single excellent mother, and yet there are many excellent daughters."

Dot didn't know if this was supposed to make her feel better. It didn't. It made her want to defend her mother, to tell this woman who was not dressed for walking in the woods and who reminded her of someone (if she could only clear her head enough to remember) that her own mother was the best mother in the world, the most loving and joyful woman who had ever existed in the whole entire world; far, far better than this stranger's mother could ever be.

"And I have no doubt at all that you are a *most* excellent daughter," the stranger went on. "My goodness, where are my manners? I should introduce myself. I am Miss Austen, and I live nearby with my mother and sister, back that way." She pointed behind her. "Now that we have talked, I believe we saw each other in London a few days ago. I hadn't expected to be able to have this further conversation with you, but I'm very glad of it."

Dot said her name was Dot, but that was all she could manage. Of course that was it—Miss Austen from the soup café. Miss Austen, as in Miss Jane Austen, the author so admired by her own mother, as in the Miss Austen whose house was a museum that she was going to visit that very afternoon. The Miss Austen who'd undoubtedly been dead for ages. *That* Miss Austen.

Miss Austen looked as if she expected a fuller introduction from Dot, but when Dot just stood there, tongue-tied, she smoothly continued, "Well, I'm delighted to meet you, Miss Dot, and I hope the rest of your walk is pleasant. I take it that your long travels are far from completed. I am quite sure that you will enjoy your path. I expect you will find it not too long, not too short, but just right. And now I must continue on my own way. Do give my greetings to your estimable aunt. Fare-thee-well, Miss Dot."

Dot watched this person who said she was Miss Austen smile, wave and walk away, not looking back. As she disappeared along the curve of the path, Dot wondered how she knew Aunt Tab. Remembering about Aunt Tab reminded Dot that she was lost.

"Damn," she said out loud, stamping a wet sneaker on the ground. It was either that or burst into tears like a baby. Get a grip, she told herself. Simmer down. What would Mom do?

Thea, she decided, would take a deep cleansing yoga breath and then carefully marshal all the facts and clues, and then the answer would come. Or at least *an* answer, one at least worth trying out. Be Inventive.

Thirteen: Lost

Dot did the same. Breathing slowly, she looked around. She saw the path, the stream, the little house with the garden and the tree swing. She went over her entire conversation with Miss Austen. What had she said about living back that way? She'd even pointed.

Bingo. Miss Austen had said she was coming from her home, and had pointed behind her. So if her home was across the road from Cassandra's Cup, as Aunt Tab had told her over breakfast, then the right path must be back that way, on the other side of where the path had split into a "T." Proud of herself for figuring this out, she turned her back on the small stone house, retraced her steps to the "T" and then set out along the other side of the path.

She had much to think about as she walked. Estimable aunt? Dot wasn't sure she knew what estimable meant, but she gathered it was a compliment. Miss Austen seemed to like to talk about the stories she was writing. Maybe she should read one. They sounded not at all like *Frankenstein.*

After about a half hour's walk, the path along the stream ended. As Dot emerged from the trees, she could hear the harsh sounds of horrible trucks grinding their gears and the high whine of fast cars. If she'd ever left it, she was now definitely back in the twenty-first century.

Her path ran directly into a highway that surely hadn't been there in Miss Austen's day. It was as bad as it could be—four lanes, a big concrete divider, lots of traffic, lots of trucks. She crouched against a small tree trunk and stared at it for a while. Every truck was a murdering Monster. She couldn't imagine crossing it. She also couldn't imagine walking alongside its narrow shoulder. Even if she could, in which direction would she go?

This was way worse than being lost in the woods.

Fourteen: Smoke Signals

Even if she had figured out which direction to take, Dot knew she could never walk along this busy highway. The shoulder was too narrow and the trucks too thick and fast. She was stuck, painfully and permanently stuck. She closed her eyes and wished for many things: to be lying on Tinkerbell on the floor of her yellow room, to be living an imaginary life in someone's happy-ending book, and most of all to re-live those minuscule moments between **BT** and **AT** that would have kept her mother standing on the sidewalk and not become her mother lying in the street.

Dot opened her eyes and looked at the sky. The clear blue of the morning was rapidly disappearing behind masses of gray clouds. It looked distressingly like the sky over the library sidewalk on that awful morning almost two months ago. Maybe if she remembered the cloud discussion she and her mother had had, word for word, she could go back in time and make it come out right. **AT** time would telescope backwards into **BT** time—Junie would say she was nuts, but Junie hadn't just met Miss Jane Austen taking a stroll in the woods. Dot closed her eyes again and deliberately thought back to those minutes right when **BT** had so mercilessly turned into **AT**.

The pain of remembering was pretty bad, even though she was doing it to herself. The tears came right though her closed eyes. When she finally opened them, she noticed that the ground around her was wetter than any amount of tears could ever have made it. And it was Hampshire dirt, not Seattle pavement that was now sopping from a heavy spring downpour. The universe had plainly decided that Dot's time travel plan

Fourteen: Smoke Signals

was a non-starter. She wiped her face, pulled up her sweatshirt hood and moved back into the woods to find some shelter.

Since she didn't really care if she lived or died, she wasn't sure why she was bothering to try to stay dry—it must be a reflex thing. As she brushed her hand on her jeans, she felt the bulge of Aunt Tab's watch in her pocket. Fishing it out, she saw it was almost noon. She was going to be late to Cassandra's Cup, assuming she got there at all, assuming she cared.

Standing unhappily under a dripping tree, holding the watch in her wet hand, Dot had to confess that her practice runaway hadn't gone so well. She'd think about that later, but now her responsible self got the upper hand and told her to concentrate on figuring out how to get to where Aunt Tab was undoubtedly already perched on a chair, tapping her bony fingers on the table, waiting for her.

Whispering "Here goes nothing," Dot stepped out from under the tree and, like a prisoner walking to the gallows, headed out toward the hideously busy highway. She forced herself to stand quietly by the roadside and take a careful look in both directions. She had to decide which way to walk, and this time no helpful historical lady came up behind her. The traffic was terrifying and the sound of the tires on the wet pavement reminded her of being on Westminster Bridge when Aunt Tab had freaked her out with the jar of her mom's ashes. That made her think of Mary Wollstonecraft jumping off the bridge into the stormy, cold water, and then her daughter growing up to write a story about a sad and murdering Monster. So much suffering and death. Bad feelings circled around Dot's hunched shoulders like a flock of impatient vultures.

Just as Dot was about to give up altogether, a small green car motored by in the slow lane, braking as it passed her. Blinking its lights, the car pulled over and stopped, blocking the narrow shoulder in front of her. Dot was about to run back into the woods when the car door opened and Mrs. Whitley heaved herself halfway out, yelping, "Young Dot, is that you? My goodness, dearie, what are you doing out in this weather? Do come here."

Dot had a hard time focusing as she walked over to the car. In as dignified a voice as she could muster, she said, "Oh, hello Mrs. Whitley. I was just out for a walk. I'm meeting my aunt at Cassandra's Cup for lunch."

"Well, you're soaking wet and going the wrong way. Get in and I'll take you there, you poor child."

Dot hated the poor child bit, but was glad to sit down in a warm dry place. She said, "Thank you, Mrs. Whitley," and slid into the passenger seat, after being confused because it was on the wrong side of the car. Wrong in every way because not only did the passenger sit on what was the driver's side in American cars, but wrong because she had to walk around to the highway side of the car, away from the safer tree and shoulder side.

After ten minutes of constant chatter, Mrs. Whitley deposited a damp Dot on the curb of an empty street with wide sidewalks. "Cheerio, dearie. There's Cassandra's Cup. Give my best to your estimable aunt."

Dot thanked Mrs. Whitley distractedly, hoping that Aunt Tab hadn't seen her arrive in a car. She had no intention of sharing her walking and navigational failures with Aunt Tab; she'd never hear the end of it. She got out and moved quickly to the inside of the sidewalk to get her bearings. It had stopped raining. Looking furtively around the quiet road, she saw a clutch of middle-aged women in pastel raincoats clustered at Cassandra's Cup's front door, just a few yards away.

Across the road, which looked more like a pedestrian-friendly wide spot than a street, was a rectangular, two-story, brick house with white trim and lots of chimneys sitting in the middle of a pleasant garden. She didn't see Aunt Tab anywhere. Maybe she was one of the ladies by the door. She started to walk over to them, skirting a stone planter full of yellow pansies, when she heard Aunt Tab's raspy voice behind her.

"Dot, sorry I'm late. Wonderful walk! How was yours?" Aunt Tab rattled on as she furled her umbrella, poking it into the pansies as she made her way to Dot's side. "Beautiful countryside. So tame, too, not like our wild Pacific Northwest mountains."

"Yeah, real tame," Dot said, trying to sound bored and dismissive. She was glad Aunt Tab didn't say anything about how wet she was.

Fourteen: Smoke Signals

"A regular storybook place around here. Thatched roofs. Smoke curling out of chimneys. Charming." Dot looked where Aunt Tab pointed. The chimney smoke reminded her of fires, which reminded her of her mother's ashes, which reminded her that Aunt Tab was carrying them around. Not charming at all. But she couldn't stop staring at it—the smoke was shifting in the wind, making pictures as it rose.

"Let's nip across the road to the Austen ladies' house first. Let these tea shop tourists thin a bit," said Aunt Tab, shaking her umbrella at the crowd around Cassandra Cup's front door and then at the brick house on the opposite side of the road.

Nip must have meant move fast, because Aunt Tab made a beeline straight across the road, as if she had the right-of-way. When she was halfway across the empty street, she looked back to see Dot, standing by the pansies, seemingly hypnotized by the rising chimney smoke.

"Dot! Over here!" Aunt Tab waved her umbrella.

Dot broke her gaze away from the smoke and shook her head at Aunt Tab.

"Sorry, not thinking." Aunt Tab muttered as she recrossed the road back to Dot. "Here, let's cross together."

Aunt Tab made exaggerated glances in both directions. "Coast is clear," she said, and aunt and niece crossed the road together.

Dot hated being such a coward, but she couldn't imagine ever crossing a street by herself. Trucks could come out of nowhere. She didn't know why she cared, though—maybe it was part of the same reflex that made her wipe raindrops off her face.

As they walked over to the Austen ladies' house, Aunt Tab launched into another round of history lectures. Dot only half listened because she was thinking about what she'd seen in the smoke. The rising smoke had curled itself into shapes, as clouds do. Dot saw a person, a traveler like an old-fashioned hobo, but dressed like a jester with pointy shoes, carrying a stick with a bandana tied on the end. As the smoke spread, the bandana became the sun and the stick a long ray of light. The traveler's feet wiggled and moved in a little breeze, as if they were dancing. At first Dot thought it was Tinkerbell, but then she wasn't so sure.

Fifteen: Miss Austen's Room

"Jane Austen lived here with her mother and sister after her father died. Her brother Edward owned the property. Jane's parents had given eleven year-old Edward away to a wealthy, childless family who needed an heir—and no one in those days thought that was a bit strange. So he inherited a lot of land around here, and in Kent, the next county over." Aunt Tab pointed her umbrella to the left. She'd apparently been studying her maps again.

That's what I need, thought Dot, somebody rich to give me their money. Then I could go wherever I wanted.

"In those days women were entirely dependent on men for their livelihoods. There wasn't any paying work women were allowed to do—the Austen ladies had no way to support themselves. No respectable way, that is. Not a happy place to be." Aunt Tab clucked her tongue disapprovingly. "A lot of what Jane Austen wrote about was how a woman could manage to find happiness in a world so stacked against her."

"Did it work out okay for Jane?"

"Mostly, but Jane was a realist. She didn't try to change the whole world like Mary Wollstonecraft did."

Assuming no rich man came along, Dot wondered what it would be like to be a grown woman and not be allowed to earn a living. What if you wanted to be an architect or a filmmaker or a doctor and you couldn't because you weren't a guy? How stupid was that? Mary Wollstonecraft's anger and frustration was starting to make sense. Dot hoped that Mary

Fifteen: Miss Austen's Room

somehow knew that her life and the books she had written had helped make everything better for future women.

But it wasn't just about not being allowed to work, Dot realized. It was also about money. At least for her, right now, that was the main thing.

She'd never thought much about money in her **BT** life. Her mother went to her job at a veterinarian's clinic, they had a house and food and clothes—no big gaps anywhere. "Enough is as good as a feast," her mother used to say happily when they ate single instead of double scoop ice cream cones. Dot had always agreed. Now she suddenly had a fleeting image of nasty Nick and the marginally nicer Nell standing in their fancy Microsoft hoodies, surrounded by piles of luggage at the airport, but nobody meeting them. They looked like they had a feast, but not of what they needed.

Maybe Dot and her mother never worried about money, and maybe everything had always worked out fine, but what about now, in motherless AT time—where would the groceries come from, not to mention ice cream cones? And what about running away? She would definitely need more than the five pounds Aunt Tab had given her at the beginning of the week.

When they reached the Austen house, Aunt Tab paid their seven pounds admission. "Isn't this money odd? All the different colors." Aunt Tab squinted as she inspected the engraving of Queen Elizabeth on the blue, five-pound note. "Too flattering by far."

The ticket clerk, overhearing, said, "Jane Austen didn't have much respect for the royal family, either. When the Prince Regent asked her to dedicate her next book to him, she refused, but very politely. When she was about your age, young lady, she wrote a history of England and came down squarely on the side of the beheaded Mary Queen of Scots over her cousin, Queen Elizabeth I. I think by the end of your visit today you will see that Miss Austen was a real person, with real opinions, not a cardboard character in a fancy dress movie."

Dot couldn't tell if the clerk was being friendly or not. Sometimes with English people it was hard to know. Most weren't as bubbly as Mrs. Whitley. Thinking about Mrs. Whitley, Dot worried again about Aunt Tab finding out that she'd been lost. Aunt Tab made her feel enough like a baby as it was. Another reason to run away.

Aunt Tab and Dot walked into the Austen ladies' house. They climbed a set of narrow, steep, and creaky wooden stairs to the small, square bedroom shared by Jane and her big sister, Cassandra. It had cream-colored wallpaper with small geometric dots. There was a black fireplace and framed quotes on the wall from famous people who loved Jane Austen's novels.

Consulting a guidebook she'd bought, Aunt Tab said, "Never had a room of her own. Not in all her forty-one years."

"That's when she died?"

"Of some disease we probably could cure today. Seems young, doesn't it? Thea's age."

"Was everyone sad? Did she have kids?"

"No, she never married. She was engaged once," Aunt Tab said after reading a little more in her guidebook, "but broke it off after twenty-four hours when she realized she wasn't willing to marry a guy she didn't love. Spunky of her. In those days, love and marriage didn't go together much. She was visiting the guy's family's house with her sister and the two women left a note and snuck away early the next morning before anyone else was up—very embarrassing. And yes, when she died, everyone who knew her was sad."

"Was she cremated?" It suddenly occurred to her that Aunt Tab might be planning to stash more of Thea's ashes behind Jane Austen's bed or something. She couldn't stand the thought of her mother being swept up by some museum housekeeper. Or what if Miss Austen herself found them?

"No, I don't think they did cremation in those days. She's buried in Winchester, the next town over, in a coffin under the aisle of a big church."

"I wouldn't like people shuffling over me all the time."

"Maybe cremation isn't such a creepy choice after all?"

Dot braced herself for the appearance of the glass jelly jar wrapped in tinfoil. But Aunt Tab just wandered around, gazing at the walls and the bed and the blue china pitcher on a little dressing table. Dot relaxed enough to take her eyes off Aunt Tab and looked around the room, too.

Fifteen: Miss Austen's Room

She noticed a quilt hanging on the wall just inside the bedroom door. It was made of scraps of colorful fabric in tiny flower patterns blooming through a latticework of polka-dotted white cotton. It looked as if the flowers were playing a game of peek-a-boo; she could almost see them waving and giggling. A large sign posted on the wall beside it said it had been pieced together by Jane and her mother. "**Do Not Touch**," the sign added in large letters.

Dot wanted to, very much.

"Hope the crowd over there is gone. Let's get lunch before it starts pouring again," said Aunt Tab, who had been looking at the darkening sky outside Jane Austen's bedroom window. "Looks as if you got caught in that morning rain yourself," she added, still gazing out the window.

Dot didn't say anything. On their way out of the bedroom, she brushed the back of her right hand against the quilt. It was soft and smooth. Although the colors and the design were completely different from *Dancing on the Edge*, both radiated the same comforting feelings. She could tell that Jane and her mother had been good friends.

"Thea once told me that Jane Austen died before she finished her last book. Jane, not your mother. Who knows how it would have ended, but your mother said it was definitely more political than her earlier books—more analytical, more critical."

"Maybe she learned something from Mary Wollstonecraft?" Dot liked when Aunt Tab told her new stuff about her mother.

"You're getting more analytical yourself," Aunt Tab said. "When you read Miss Austen, you will find it impossible not to notice that all her heroines are quite independent-thinking young women."

"Why was she so interested in girls with useless mothers?"

"How do you know that?"

Dot didn't answer. She remembered she wanted to look up "estimable."

They walked back down the creaky stairs and into the gift shop. Aunt Tab bought a tea towel with the names of Jane Austen's six books printed on it, a postcard of her desk, and a stamp. Dot looked at a display of quill pens and thought it would be very hard to write a school paper, let alone a whole novel, with such crude, scratchy implements. She wondered what Jane thought about having all these strangers trooping through her house.

"Which Jane Austen book should I read first?" she asked the woman behind the counter, who, like everyone else in the house, was dressed in the long skirts and shawls of Jane's day.

"What a good question. I envy you young people who are reading Jane for the first time," the woman sighed, patting her white cap. "If you have enough money for two, I'd suggest *Pride and Prejudice* because it's so fun, and *Persuasion* because it's so beautifully thoughtful."

Dot remembered her mom had said *Pride and Prejudice* was the one to start with. She decided to splurge and buy both. Sometimes a feast was the right choice.

Sixteen: Sugar Bowl

Walking outside with her new Jane Austen books, Dot found Aunt Tab leaning against a brick wall, writing her postcard. "To your teacher," she explained. "I told Mr. Cyrus we'd keep in touch."

She dropped the card in a cylindrical red postbox and together they crossed the empty road, neither saying anything about the clouds crowding the sky above them. Dot told herself that she didn't care what Aunt Tab had written to Mr. Cyrus.

The line at the door of Cassandra's Cup was gone and they were immediately ushered inside by a young woman in polka-dotted, high-waisted Austen attire who took them to a small corner table by a window. The pastel café walls were banded with plate rails at eye level that displayed decorated cups and saucers, milk pitchers and sugar bowls, all for sale.

"Charming place," Aunt Tab commented, but Dot thought she was being sarcastic. It was a little over the top, like Mrs. Whitley's house. They looked at their menus, which, like the fish and chips place, was full of foods they didn't recognize. "Don't remember all these in the guidebooks. Wonder what a 'Toasted Wig' is? These English get funnier and funnier."

Aunt Tab decided on the mulligatawny soup and Dot asked for a cheese and bacon sandwich. They easily agreed on Earl Grey tea. The waitress swept away in her long muslin dress.

"So how was your walk?" asked Aunt Tab, fiddling with her napkin.

"Fine," said Dot. No way was she going to talk about being lost, and even less about meeting Jane Austen. If that's what had happened. She didn't want to talk about that part because, well, because it was private.

Sixteen: Sugar Bowl

Strange and private. She wasn't even sure she'd have talked to her mother about it, which was an odd thought to have.

Quietly drinking her tea, Dot came to a couple of conclusions about her practice runaway. First, it hadn't gone too well. It was possible that reading *Frankenstein* wasn't the best preparation for a walk in the woods where you've never been before. It was also possible that she shouldn't plan to run away without a GPS. Either that, or only run away to cities with street signs. Except cities had all those sidewalks and trucks. That was a problem.

Overshadowing it all, though, was the second thought: If she had truly met Jane Austen, back from the dead in a much nicer way than Victor Frankenstein's Monster, why wouldn't it be possible for her mother to come back, too?

This was a gigantic thought, and Dot was afraid to think about it directly, like not looking at the sun. It was a fantastic thought, silly and babyish, too. But on the other hand, weren't strange things happening? Maybe past and present weren't as separate as most people think. Maybe life and death aren't as separate, either? Mr. Cyrus sometimes talked about history as if it were still happening—yesterday and today's wars and famous people from all the centuries mixed up together.

Dot snuck a look at Aunt Tab. She was craning around in her seat, as if she were looking for something. Or someone. Could she talk about any of this with her? Maybe Aunt Tab wasn't being such a total dork anymore, but she was so *not* Thea, and besides, Dot just had this feeling that she needed to figure this (whatever the "this" was) out on her own.

She wished Junie were here. She really wanted to get on Mrs. Whitley's computer as soon as they got back.

Their food arrived in the midst of this tricky thinking. Dot noticed with surprise that she felt truly hungry, and that her sandwich looked even more appetizing than the fish and chips the night before. The cheese melting through the little holes in her toasted bread looked and smelled yummy, and she could see bacon pieces in between. She gave the pickle that was on the side of her plate to Aunt Tab and picked up her sandwich.

"Never liked pickles? Me neither," Aunt Tab said, putting Dot's pickle back on Dot's plate. "Your mother was the only pickle-eater in the house when we were growing up. You never know, though. Pickles might be better in Hampshire."

The sandwich was good. The cheese was sharper and tastier than American cheese, and it wasn't bright yellow. In fact, some of the yellow that she'd seen coming through the toasted holes was mustard, not cheese. And the bacon was that thick and limp English kind, more like ham. She ate it slowly, enjoying it like she used to enjoy food. Even the bread had flavor and was chewy and crunchy in the toasted parts.

When she finished, she picked up her pickle and took a tiny bite.

"When you're ready, we have a job to do," said Aunt Tab, looking pointedly at her bag, which was draped over the back of her chair.

Dot knew what she was talking about but wasn't so freaked out about it now. Maybe touching the quilt had helped. Or maybe it was tasting the pickle, which wasn't as bad as she'd expected. She nodded and waited for Aunt Tab's idea about this second ash deposit.

"Scattering them in Miss Austen's garden is trite. We need something more interesting. What do you think?" Aunt Tab picked up the teapot and poured herself another cup of Earl Grey.

Dot hadn't expected to have a say, but an image came to her almost immediately.

"Something to do with tea," said Dot. "And sugar. Mom loved tea with one sugar cube. Once we did a science project where we dripped tea onto sugar cubes on the kitchen counter. Slowly, off a spoon handle, drop by drop, just until the cube started to crumble. We counted how many drops it took to dissolve the cube. Some cubes could hold more than others before they fell apart but the average was ten. Usually the cubes leaked tea out the bottom before the sides collapsed. We experimented with dropping the tea from different heights and that made a difference, too."

"You won a prize that year, didn't you?"

"Yeah, second prize. I made a big poster and had cubes all lined up with different numbers of drops having been dripped on them and figured out the averages and stuff."

Sixteen: Sugar Bowl

Dot fell silent as the **BT** memories took over. She was back in her kitchen at home, the blue Formica counter sticky with little piles of tea-stained sugar, her mother laughing as Dot dripped the tea from different heights, standing on a kitchen chair. After they'd done their counting and observing and recording, Thea had scraped up the remains to stir into her tea.

"Well then, let's open one of these silly sugar bowls on the rail behind you and sprinkle in some of Thea's ashes. Someday someone will buy it and *quelle surprise!*" Aunt Tab laughed as if this were the best joke in the world.

Dot wasn't sure it was *that* funny, but she did think the idea had possibilities. The main thing was, what would Thea think? She'd like the tea and sugar part, for sure. She might even appreciate the fact that it happened in a restaurant named for Jane Austen's big sister—a kind of backhanded thank you to Tab for taking over teaching Dot about her names and the three ladies.

But what about the fact that whoever eventually bought the sugar bowl would inevitably open the lid and throw out the sandy stuff inside? How could that be a good thing? Most of the customers here were Jane Austen fans visiting from all over the world. So the sugar bowl could end up anywhere, which Dot knew Thea would like: the journey's not over; maybe it's never quite over. But she wished there were a way to make the buyer save the ash, and not throw it out at all.

"Here's the icing on the cake," cackled Aunt Tab, as if she could read Dot's mind. "We put a note in the bowl that says:

"Valuable Souvenir Mount St. Helens Volcanic Ash."

Dot had to hand it to Aunt Tab. Talk about being inventive.

"How could we do it? There's people all around."

Aunt Tab leaned across the table and whispered conspiratorially, "I'll write the note. You pick out a bowl, take it down and hand it to me, like we're thinking of buying it. You keep watch and I'll do the deed."

Dot remembered her mother laughing at the kitchen counter. She remembered the smile and the kind words of the woman who said she was Jane Austen. She remembered two beautiful mother-daughter sewing projects.

"Let's do it," she said.

Seventeen: Good Stuff, Bad Stuff

Dot reached up to take down a pale green sugar bowl. It was the largest and least silly looking of the three that were lined up on the plate rail behind her. She examined it carefully, holding it in both hands, trying to look like a potential buyer of a pale green sugar bowl.

"What do you think of this one, Aunt Tab?" she said in a stagey voice, handing it across to her aunt.

Aunt Tab took the sugar bowl in her left hand and turned it this way and that, eyeing it carefully. With her right hand, she fumbled in her bag for the ash jar.

"I'm trying not to look like a shoplifter," Aunt Tab whispered to Dot.

Dot smiled crookedly and tried to provide a little covering banter, talking about how good the Earl Grey tea was. She stood up, pretending to look at the other bowls on the rail, shielding Aunt Tab's nefarious activity from prying eyes.

Aunt Tab found the jelly jar and put it in her lap. She untwisted the lid with one hand, an awkward move that spilled a spoonful of ash on her napkin. Dot gulped as she saw it lying there, granular and a little sparkly on Aunt Tab's lap. "Oops, sorry, Thea," Aunt Tab said, and quickly poured the remaining quarter cup from the jar into the sugar bowl. Then she dropped in the note "Valuable Souvenir Mount St. Helens Volcanic Ash." She gathered the last little bits off her napkin and salted them over the top. Making a final show of caressing the bowl's curving double handles, she replaced the top and smoothly handed it to Dot, who returned it to the ledge, but not quite as smoothly.

"No, I think not. Not quite the right color," Aunt Tab said, a little too loudly.

Dot nodded, but couldn't speak. She felt a little dizzy and sat down quickly, taking a few deep breaths.

Aunt Tab put on a face that Dot tried to copy—the face of a shopper who'd regretfully changed her mind. Then they finished their tea, after ceremonially adding extra sugar to their cups. Dot took another bite of pickle.

"You'd make a terrible thief," Aunt Tab said to Dot as they walked out of Cassandra's Cup into the rainy afternoon.

"You too," said Dot. It had been kind of fun, actually, and she could almost hear her mother's voice saying, "Awesome job, Miss Dorothy Mary-Jane," like she had whenever she saw Dot do something hard.

They walked back to Mrs. Whitley's along Aunt Tab's route, which was a sidewalk that ran along a quiet residential road with no trucks and only a few cars. It should have been, well, if not entirely pleasant, at least okay. But it wasn't.

Every time Dot started to feel better, something happened to knock her down. A sight, a memory, a thought, and it was like an invisible hand flipped an invisible toggle and her feeling-better mood switched off. She trailed behind, not sharing Aunt Tab's umbrella, scuffing her wet sneakers along the pavement, hiding from the world under her jacket hood, occupied with sad thoughts about Mary's *Frankenstein* story.

Elizabeth, Victor's foster sister and true love, was a smart girl, but Victor wouldn't tell her that he'd created a troublesome Monster, so there was no way Elizabeth could help him or do anything to save herself. A friend of theirs was framed for the murder of Victor's little brother. Victor knew the Monster was the real murderer, but was afraid to tell anyone about the Monster's existence, so the innocent friend was hanged for it. Elizabeth, not knowing about the Monster, but convinced that their friend could not possibly be guilty, said to Victor, *"When falsehood can look so like the truth, who can assure themselves of certain happiness? I feel as if I were walking on the edge of a precipice..."*

That's how Dot felt—every curb was the edge of a precipice, she was definitely very confused about what was true, and she certainly had no assurance of happiness. Dot totally understood Elizabeth's point of view.

Elizabeth, though, had ended up dead.

Nineteen-year-old Mary had written a complicated book that made Dot's feelings ricochet back and forth, first feeling sympathetic toward Victor and then toward the Monster. Running through the story was Mary's suggestion that the Monster could have been entirely different—a scary looking creature for sure, but, if people had been nice to him, he might not have been so evil. Then there was the whole idea hanging out there about bringing the dead to life; Dot found that concept understandably attractive.

But the story also appealed to her for the opposite reason. Its gloomy ending perfectly matched the worst of her **AT** moods—nothing comes out right at the end, and everyone dies. No, she remembered, not quite everyone. Felix and Agatha's poverty-stricken family in the hut, after they beat up the Monster and ran away, they came out alright. That gave the book even more tricky layers—good and bad weren't always rewarded or punished as a reader might want. Like real life, Dot guessed.

She liked the Mary part of her name more and more. It could be for Mary Wollstonecraft and for her daughter, Mary, too—mother and daughter then, mother and daughter now.

She walked faster to catch up with Aunt Tab. "Why did the daughter Mary write *Frankenstein*? Had something bad happened to her, too?"

"Well, yes and no. Depends."

"Aunt Tab, don't talk like that! You know what I mean."

"Okay, the bad stuff: Mary Wollstonecraft, her mother, died eleven days after she gave birth to her in 1797. Baby Mary was farmed around for a while and then raised by a step-mother who didn't much like her. Some good stuff: Her father loved her, in between being a busy political revolutionary. When the young poet and political radical Shelley, who was twenty

Seventeen: Good Stuff, Bad Stuff

years old, came to visit her father, he and sixteen-year-old Mary fell in love. Shelley also thought Mary's mother's *A Vindication of the Rights of Woman* was one of the best books ever written.

"More bad stuff: Shelley was already married and had two kids. Good stuff, maybe: He and daughter Mary loved each other so much that they ran away and she got pregnant. Bad stuff: The baby died. Good stuff: A little while later, she got pregnant again and this baby lived. They were very happy. They went to Switzerland with some friends, and then to Italy to write and make a new life for themselves. Shelley and Mary and one of those friends, another great poet named Byron, decided to have a contest to see who could write the best gothic novel. Mary wrote *Frankenstein* and neither Shelley nor Byron finished anything." Aunt Tab sniffed at the men's failure, and shook the rain off her umbrella.

It took Dot a couple of blocks of walking to sort out all of Mary's running around. Nowadays when teenagers had babies and ran away and weren't married, it was considered a bad thing. People either tried to stop them, or else they gave up and didn't even try to help them. Mostly it happened to kids who didn't have any money or were into drugs and had dropped out of school, and mostly the girls didn't have mothers who'd written famous books, and great writers didn't fall in love with them, and they didn't go on to write famous books themselves while they were nursing new babies while still being teenagers. This was different. Why had times changed?

Or had they? Maybe there was another Mary Wollstonecraft Shelley out there right now.

"I forgot to mention that besides being a great poet and a political radical, Shelley was also very, very rich. That makes a difference," Aunt Tab said.

Dot agreed. Running away would be a lot easier if she had a rich friend.

Eighteen: Somebody Has to Push

Dot and Aunt Tab arrived on Mrs. Whitley's tiny front porch just as the rain increased to heavy pounding spikes. "Good timing," said Aunt Tab, congratulating herself. Mrs. Whitley wasn't around, which was good because then she couldn't blab to Aunt Tab about finding poor bedraggled Dot by the roadside, but it was bad because Dot desperately wanted to check her email and send Junie a note.

Dot stuffed her daypack in the bottom of her suitcase, after first checking to make sure her passport was there and relatively dry. Reassured, she then ran her hands across *Dancing on the Edge,* fingering the boat with the stitched words, *Be Daring*. That was meant for Mary Wollstonecraft, she now knew. Next was the house by the road with the garden and the words, *Be Inventive*. That was for Jane Austen. She'd start reading *Pride and Prejudice* next, she decided. But she wasn't done with the two Marys yet.

"How much was Mary Shelley like her mother?" she asked Aunt Tab as she returned to Mrs. Whitley's small living room, where her aunt was eating from a plate of biscuits left by Mrs. Whitley.

"Tough question," she said, wiping crumbs off her chin. Aunt Tab had certainly adapted to the English way of eating. "Quite a lot in some ways, but very different in others. It's hard to say because they never got to know each other in person. By the way, Mary Shelley is Mary Shelley because she and Shelley did finally marry—a few months after Shelley's first wife drowned herself in London."

"Jesus, Aunt Tab, this isn't history. This is HBO."

Eighteen: Somebody Has to Push

"I don't agree with Thea letting you swear like that. But to your question—in their strengths, the mother and daughter were very similar, and that's what Thea was thinking of when she named you. Both Marys thought long and hard before they decided something, and once decided, they made no secret of it. I'm talking about big things here, not what are you going to wear tomorrow, but more like what are you going to believe in and then what are you going to do about it. Following other people was not their thing. They were independent thinkers. People who live their principles like they did have to be daring because they never take the easy way out."

Dot liked this part. "What else?"

"Two things mainly, and your mother believed these, too. First, neither Mary believed that because things are the way they are, then that's the way they will always be. A person's life never has only one way it can go. And secondly, both Marys believed that anyone, including themselves, could make the future different from the past and better than the present."

Aunt Tab firmly bit into another biscuit. "Change doesn't just happen. Somebody has to push. Doesn't mean you're always right, but if you don't try, you'll never find out."

"Sounds like Mr. Cyrus. He's always talking about how history is just people like us who got up and did something. Sometimes the something causes big problems like it's a dictator or a killer or a crazy person, and sometimes the something is helpful, like inventors or artists or scientists. But they're all just people. And even if you're not one of them, every single one of us needs to be smart enough to pick who to follow and who not to—"

"*Whom* to follow, not *who*," Aunt Tab interrupted. "But you're right. Takes two to tango. Smart man, that Mr. Cyrus, and good for you for listening to him. Did he also say that changing the future is hard work, and that a person may not live to see it?"

"Maybe. I don't remember that part," Dot said, not wanting to talk about people not living. "I'm going to go read *Pride and Prejudice*."

"I'll stay out of your way, then. I have some knitting to tend to."

An image of the Monster's skin, stitched together like knitting, flitted through Dot's brain. She didn't know that Aunt Tab was a knitter.

"And, Dot, don't forget that tomorrow we head up to the Lake District."

• • •

Aunt Tab came to bed after Dot was already asleep. She'd staked out her half of the bed, running a rolled-up extra blanket down the middle, hoping it would keep Aunt Tab's jittery limbs from bumping into her. It must have worked, because Dot slept well and when she woke up, Aunt Tab was sleeping quite linearly on her side of the bed.

Dot dressed quietly and went into Mrs. Whitley's breakfast room, carrying *Pride and Prejudice*.

"Well, good morning, dearie. Up with the birds, are we? I don't have breakfast quite ready yet."

"Hello, Mrs. Whitley," said Dot, opening up the book, hoping to avoid more of that sort of conversation. "I'm not hungry anyway."

"Where's your lovely auntie? Sleeping the sleep of the just, is she?"

"I guess so. Say, Mrs. Whitley, I'd appreciate it if you didn't mention about finding me on that road."

"Mum's the word, young Dot. It's our secret. I know how these things can be."

"Thanks," said Dot, doubting that Mrs. Whitley had any idea of how these things can be. She was glad that Mrs. Whitley was being so agreeable, but she didn't want to pay for it by becoming her best friend. "Could I use your computer to check my email?"

"Of course you can, little Dot. We're all up to date here in Alton. Come along, take as much time as you need."

Junie had written back.

```
Hiya, time travel, sure, why not. Happens in
the movies all the time. Remember when we
used to pretend we lived in a movie? Maybe
pretending can turn into real. Like when
```

Eighteen: Somebody Has to Push

your mom said if you smile pretending to be
happy pretty soon you really will be happy.

Still thinking about running away?
BFF
Junie

Dot didn't remember her mother ever saying that. She also wasn't so sure it was true.

Junie, YES I am still thinking about running away. I stole my passport out of Aunt Tab's suitcase. Passport but no plan. Wish you were here—I got lost in the woods and was saved by Jane Austen. Really. And she's been dead, whatever that means, for 200 years. She's really nice. She and her mom made a quilt like my mom and I made. There was a sign that said don't touch, but I did, just a little.

Aunt Tab is being totally unpredictable—sometimes she's OK and sometimes I can't wait to get away from her. The other day I think I laughed for the first time. It felt weird, like I didn't know if it was OK or not. Wish you were here. I know I said that before. It's hard having only grown-ups to talk to.

```
Tell Mr. Cyrus I'm running into a lot of
history here, and it's even messier than
he thinks.

Gotta go,
DMJ

PS: Did I tell you about the ash part? We
really are leaving my Mom's ashes in dif-
ferent places—in a restaurant yesterday. At
first I thought it was crazy and bad, but
now I kinda get it. But it's hard having
to say good-bye over and over.
```

Dot closed down the session and went back to the bedroom, where Aunt Tab was still sleeping soundly in her half of the bed. She went in to Mrs. Whitley's living room to read *Pride and Prejudice* for a while. Miss Austen's book had some funny moments, but it wasn't gripping her like *Frankenstein*. It began with a very silly and useless mother, just as Jane Austen had said. There were five sisters and at first it was hard to keep them all straight. A few appeared to be excellent, but not all of them. After reading ten or fifteen pages, Dot heard Aunt Tab rattling down the hall toward the breakfast table, so she marked her place in the book and went to join her.

The table was once again spread with the predictable fixings of a Full English Breakfast and Aunt Tab did her usual excellent imitation of a hungry English person. Dot picked at a dry cereal called Weetabix. Her appetite had dropped back to its normal never-hungry AT levels.

"We need to stop at a bookstore in London, between our trains," Aunt Tab said, her mouth full of gross baked beans and toast. "I need another guidebook for the Lake District. We're going to take a hike there."

"Whatever," said Dot. She was thinking about her mother's ashes in the sugar bowl. Like she'd told Junie, saying good-bye so many times was

Eighteen: Somebody Has to Push

hard. On the other hand, Thea had always wanted to travel, but had never had the chance. Dot hadn't realized that England was so special a place for her, but obviously it was, with all these women being from here. So it was probably a good thing to be doing this. Maybe, too, it was a reason to stay in England when she ran away, instead of going home.

She wished her running-away plans were less slushy. So far they weren't nearly solid enough. Like the difference between a damp pile of loose sugar and a hard, dry sugar cube. The idea of running away to stay in England sounded increasingly cool to her. If her mom had liked England enough to name her after three Englishwomen, then maybe that was a message that she should be there. Be here.

As she smashed her Weetabix into the cardboardy mush it really was, she liked the idea more and more, assuming she could learn to recognize edible food. Which Weetabix clearly wasn't. And assuming she could solve the money problem.

"I think I'll finish packing," Dot said, getting up from the table. She wanted to get her passport back into her jeans pocket.

"Good plan. Our train leaves in an hour, and it'll take twenty minutes to walk to the station and buy our tickets. I'll finish breakfast and say good-bye to Mrs. Whitley. Then I'll be in to finish my packing, too." Sometimes Aunt Tab seemed to need to talk out everything she was going to do.

Later, when Aunt Tab banged through the bedroom door, Dot watched nervously as she tossed things into her suitcase. Fortunately, she remained true to her untidy self, and didn't bother to straighten anything out or check for details like passports. "All set?" she asked Dot.

Dot folded the cool silk of *Dancing on the Edge* so that Jane Austen's house was on top, and laid it in her suitcase. Then she scrunched Tink's sticking-out arm into a corner and zipped it shut.

"Ready when you are," she said to Aunt Tab, patting her passport, reassuringly hidden in her back jeans pocket.

Part III: Decisions

Nineteen: Nick-spotting

Aunt Tab shouted one last good-bye to the ever-cheery Mrs. Whitley as she and Dot bumped their suitcases noisily across the cement lily pads out to the sidewalk. The sky had cleared and an eddying spring breeze set Mrs. Whitley's plastic whirligigs spinning in all directions. Dot took her usual worried look up and down the street and then positioned herself on the far inside of the sidewalk. One good thing about Miss Austen's *Pride and Prejudice* was that there were no cars or trucks in the scenery. No murdering Monsters, either. So far.

On the train back to London's Waterloo Station, Aunt Tab dozed a bit and Dot mostly stared out the window, watching the green countryside gradually lose out to concrete and tall buildings. When they arrived at Track 6, they learned they had to go to a different train station, called Euston, on the other side of London to catch their train to Penrith, the stop nearest Dorothy Wordsworth's Lake District home in the far northwest of the country. Dot didn't know there were cities with more than one train station. Compared to London, Seattle was small in space and short on time.

"This might work," Dot said as they studied a large, colored Tube map on Waterloo's tiled wall. "Look, the Northern Line will take us straight to Euston Station, no change needed. And we don't have to cross any streets."

"Good pathfinding," said Aunt Tab. "And we'll have time to find lunch and a Lake District hiking guide before our train leaves."

Dot liked riding the Tube. Once they'd made it down the flights of stairs and around the corners and onto the train, it was easy to sit quietly

Nineteen: Nick-spotting

and be taken where you needed to go, all underground without having to face any traffic at all.

"Stay here with our bags while I find the ticket seller," Aunt Tab said when they walked into the cavernous Euston Station. It was bigger than Waterloo; there were pigeons flying around, and lots of people with suitcases and backpacks. Some people carried hiking boots and walking sticks. Dot wondered if they were going to the same place she was. Aunt Tab had said that the Lake District was big hiking country.

Dot and her mother had never done any real hiking, but occasionally they'd gone up to the foothills of the Cascades and rambled along paths that looped around lakes or up and down small ridges. Dot had loved it, but then she loved everything she'd done with Thea. Her mother knew all the birds and trees and made everything magical and fun. Dot's solo walk to Cassandra's Cup had been a mini-hike, too, but the trees were all different and she'd never been lost with her mother. And, as far as she knew, they'd never run into any dead women.

Aunt Tab returned, clutching their train tickets, and they trundled their bags outside to find a bookstore and a place to get lunch. Being on big city streets again was tough, and Dot was relieved when they found a medium-sized bookstore with large front windows less than a block away. As Aunt Tab searched out the best Lake District guidebook, Dot wandered along the crowded shelves and thought about bookstores and libraries. She preferred libraries. They were quieter and had more books, and the books were sturdier and shabbier, like they'd been through a lot and could take even more. But she wasn't sure she'd ever walk through a library door again.

Turning down the poetry aisle, she saw a boy sitting on the floor against the wall at the end, reading a book. He had on a gray tee shirt and faded jeans. His dark curly hair covered his ears. He looked at her briefly with bright blue eyes and then returned to his book. It was Nick, the nasty boy from the airplane.

She turned around quickly and hurried back to the front of the store where the travel guides were. What an awful coincidence. Maybe she didn't want to stay in England after all. At least he didn't seem to have recognized her. She hurriedly told Aunt Tab that she'd wait outside. Halfway out the bookstore door, she stopped. She couldn't possibly wait outside. Being by herself on a city sidewalk next to a very busy street was the last thing in the world she was capable of doing. The second she went out there by herself, she knew she'd see her mother's body, draped in that impossible way over the curb, and the world would come to a stop again and she couldn't bear it. And those London buses were all red, red all over, and they were everywhere.

She retreated to the safety of a magazine stand back inside the store, across from the cash registers. She gazed fixedly at the magazines to recover her balance. There was a poetry journal right at her eye level. "Revisiting Coleridge" was the lead story. Weird—Coleridge again.

"Let's eat," said Aunt Tab, tapping Dot on her shoulder with her new Lake District hiking book. As they walked out the door together, Aunt Tab added, "Odd, but I think that rude, nasty boy from the plane was in line behind me. He was buying a poetry book. Coleridge."

Dot didn't reply and Aunt Tab was already on to finding a lunch place.

Twenty: The Star of Alethea

The train from London north to Penrith was a four-hour ride. It poured rain all during the middle half. Dot enjoyed watching the storm sweep over the open fields to the west and then disappear in the distance on the other side of the train. The skies had gone from dark blue to purple to gray and yellow and then to a watery blue, like heavy undulating curtains being drawn across the horizon. Dot wondered if it was a little like Junie's parents' Northern Lights.

By the time they pulled into Penrith, the air was pale and the earth was dark from all the soaked-up water. They got off the train with a crowd of hikers, and learned that they needed to catch a bus to Keswick, which was the town everyone was going to. The bus stop for Keswick was conveniently located right outside the train station's front door. Aunt Tab picked up a pamphlet about Keswick from a tourist rack as they followed the hikers outside to the brick turnaround to wait for the bus.

Dot wasn't sure she was capable of standing at a bus stop, but this wasn't directly on the road and it didn't look at all like the city bus stop in front of the Seattle Library. To help keep the memories at bay, she focused on the landscape and the scenery.

Considering all the hikers coming here, it didn't look like what she would consider good hiking territory. No tall mountains or rocky crags in sight. Some rounded hills, some rock faces, but nothing very wild looking. Lots of sheep, too, in grassy fields, with heather and low stone walls. She didn't know why it was called the Lake District—she hadn't seen any lakes

Twenty: The Star of Alethea

yet. It was pretty, though. It made sense that Dorothy Wordsworth and her brother and Coleridge would have liked living here.

"There used to be a train that went all the way, but not anymore," said one of the hikers to Aunt Tab. "Wordsworth would have been glad the train stopped coming to Keswick. He hated tourists."

"He means William, Dorothy's brother," explained Aunt Tab to Dot.

After a few minutes, a half-sized bus dieseled to a shuddering stop in front of them. It was nondescript beige, not at all threatening. A cardboard sign propped in the front window said "KESWICK." As soon as they sat down, Aunt Tab started reading aloud from the tourist brochure, which Dot thought was rude to the other passengers. The whole bus couldn't escape learning that Keswick had been settled since 500 A.D., and that the Romans had been there, as well as Norse invaders. "A lot of time under that bridge," Aunt Tab said approvingly.

"That's our stone circle." The bus driver pointed off to the left just as Aunt Tab was reading about it, "Five thousand years old, older than Stonehenge." It didn't look like much to Dot—a bunch of gray stones, like lumpy old washing machines arranged in a big circle on a grassy field. Still, it was cool that it was so old.

Aunt Tab continued her recitation, reading that Keswick had a farmers' market every week going all the way back to 1276. That reminded Dot of the Saturday farmer's market near her house. It was in the parking lot of a school and was always jam-packed with people. It was more than a place to buy food—people met their friends there, and kids played, and farmers handed out samples and helped backyard gardeners who had questions about their own lettuces or tomatoes. Everyone in Seattle obsessed over tomatoes because the summers were never quite hot enough or long enough to reliably grow the really good ones. Everyone traded stories about what they'd tried—special locations, exotic seed varieties, different pruning techniques. Her mother called homegrown tomatoes the local Holy Grail. Dot used to love tomatoes. But not AT. Except maybe the yellow ones.

"Twelve seventy-six, think of all those centuries between then and now! Wonder where our DNA was back then, eh, Dot? Could have been right here in the Lake District, in the body of some invading Norse woman. It's all still there, you know, our inherited DNA, in every cell, copying itself from person to person ever since the first human and even back into apes and chimpanzees."

Dot turned away from Aunt Tab to let her know she was being creepy again, and watched the green and heathery English countryside go by. Aunt Tab was right about one thing—the 1200s was a long time ago. Odd that this place had been civilized all that time and it still wasn't covered with strip malls, suburbs, freeways, or skyscrapers. Not even very many roads. Just small grassy fields and farmhouses with hills in the distance, heading toward what the brochure said was a pretty lakeside town of five thousand people. Not the way history happened in America, Dot was fairly sure of that. She remembered Mr. Cyrus's unit on urban sprawl and how it combined the worst of living in a city with the worst of living in the suburbs. This was way better. England definitely had its good points.

Rumbling down a narrow, twisty street, the bus came to a stop in front of a grocery store parking lot. As they wrestled their stuff off the bus, Dot glanced at the nearby streets and found them much less intimidating than London, and friendlier looking than in Alton. Fewer cars, no trucks so far, and the sidewalks were wide. The buildings were unthreatening pale colors and only a couple of stories tall. Best yet, there appeared to be whole streets with cement posts in them and signs saying, "Pedestrians Only." Now *that* was a good idea!

"Where are we staying, Aunt Tab?"

"Don't know yet. Thought we'd figure it out when we arrived. More fun that way. See the Tourist Information Center sign up there? Spelled C-e-n-t-r-e, of course. Let's go ask."

The tourist office information clerk, an officious woman in a baggy brown skirt and bulky sweater, scolded Aunt Tab and said she was doubtful anything would be available.

Twenty: The Star of Alethea

"You should have booked ahead. Tourist season never ends nowadays. Half come for the hiking and half for our literary sights."

Aunt Tab stood her ground quietly, looking at the map of the area spread out under the glass counter top. Hotels and pubs were marked, as well as all the tourist attractions. Dot noticed there were two Wordsworth houses and a Coleridge one. And there was a lake, too, called Derwentwater.

Seeing that her customers weren't moving, the clerk sighed and turned to make a few calls. On the third try, she found there had been a cancellation at a nearby pub that had a few overnight rooms. It was called The Star of Alethea. She circled the location on a folded town map and gave it to Aunt Tab, along with another lecture about how responsible tourists call ahead.

A couple of blocks away, they found The Star of Alethea. It was a low, rambling, pasted-together building featuring, so the sign out front proclaimed, "Turkish-Greek-Indian Cuisine—The Best in the Lakes." The young receptionist told them how lucky they were to get a room, and if they wanted dinner, the pub served food for only another hour.

"Thank you, dearie," said Aunt Tab and they went off to find their room, which turned out to be an adventurous trek through a maze of stairs, sharp turns, and three sets of swinging doors. When they made it to their room, Dot noted approvingly that it had two beds. She unpacked Tinkerbell and laid her on one of the beds, and unfolded *Dancing on the Edge* and draped it over a mirror. Aunt Tab got excited when she noticed they could see a sliver of Keswick's lake, Derwentwater, from their window. "Coleridge named one of his sons Derwent," she said.

Retracing their steps back to the lobby, including a few wrong turns, they found The Star of Alethea's pub packed with noisy hikers. "Hate noisy restaurants," Aunt Tab said, and herded Dot back out. They walked outside and down the pedestrian-only street, passing several other eateries that didn't appeal to Aunt Tab either. They ended up at the bottom of the street, by the grocery store where the bus had dropped them off.

"Let's make us a picnic," Aunt Tab said, and so they wandered the grocery aisles, admiring the huge array of jams, marmalades, and jellies, and puzzling over something gross-looking called Marmite. They settled on Greek yogurt, seeded rolls, a small round of cheese with a picture of Wallace and Gromit on the label, two apples, a carton of grapefruit juice, and a rolled chocolate cake. "Normal food," observed Dot, giving their collection her blessing. They took it back to their room and ate it with the window open. The fresh air helped Dot's appetite and then made her sleepy. She went to bed early, snuggled under Tinkerbell, thinking this part of England had gotten itself off on the perfectly right foot.

Twenty-One: Less Drama Is Better

Dot awoke next morning to see sunshine cloaking the creamy stone buildings across the street from her Star of Alethea window. Just beyond, the brown peaks of the fells, which is what Aunt Tab said the English around here called hills (more language weirdness: in Miss Austen's Hampshire, she'd told her that the hills there were called downs), radiated the subtle glow of milk chocolate, and between their tops, the valleys hummed with friendly sheep munching bright, spring-green grass. Dot craned her neck around the edge of the window to see the glinting sapphire patch of Derwentwater spreading south from the town. Just across the lake, she could see the rocky top of a fell. She unfolded Aunt Tab's map on the floor by her bed and figured out that the hill was called Catbells. She liked the name.

She'd had a cat once, but not for very long, because she turned out to be allergic to them. She and her mother had spent a lot of time talking about what to name the cat, a gray-and-brown-striped male from the pound. After living with him for a few days, they'd named him Huck after Huckleberry Finn, because the cat was clever and self-reliant. The next day, Dot broke out in a terrible rash and her eyes wouldn't stop watering, so they had to give Huck away.

Dot still occasionally thought about Huck, and now, seeing Catbells on the map, she remembered that her mother had tied a little bell around his neck. She looked out the window again at the fell named Catbells and smiled, a little.

Twenty-One: Less Drama Is Better

"What are you smiling about?" Aunt Tab said from her bed. "Good sign. Dorothy Wordsworth must be working her magic. Time to get a move on."

• • •

"Now we come to Dorothy," Aunt Tab said seriously as they stood in line for the Full English Breakfast downstairs in The Star of Alethea's dining room. Dot stayed away from the Weetabix and Aunt Tab told her to try a toast-and-bacon sandwich. "Miss Wordsworth is the most puzzling of all three of your ladies. It's your first name and I hope you know you have the same birthday, but I don't think that's the whole reason. We have homework to do."

Dot let her go on. Dorothy Wordsworth lived longer than either Mary Wollstonecraft or Jane Austen, but had left fewer marks on the world. As Aunt Tab told it, Dorothy Wordsworth's story was not nearly as exciting as the Marys, and only a little more adventurous than Jane Austen's.

Dorothy Wordsworth and her brother William had lived together in this remote and isolated Lake District for most of their lives, even after William got married and had a family. William was yet another great poet who revolutionized English poetry, even before Shelley. Dorothy Wordsworth idolized her brother and always made sure he had the warmest, most comfortable room in the house. Then she would tiptoe quietly around cooking and cleaning and not disturbing his great work. While he napped, she copied out his poems in drafty rooms by candlelight in her neat handwriting so publishers could read them. Didn't sound like much of a life.

Dorothy Wordsworth also took many long walks in the Lake District hills and valleys, and she kept a diary about her life. Aunt Tab said the diary wasn't about herself as much as it was about the beauty and power of the trees and rocks and plants and weather. Some of Dorothy's descriptions of nature mysteriously made their way, word for word, into her brother's famous poems. She knew it, and Aunt Tab said she didn't mind a bit.

William and Coleridge (who always went by his last name) were great friends for a time and wrote a book of poems together in 1798—the year after Mary Wollstonecraft had baby Mary—that changed poetry forever.

Dot gathered that poetry mattered a lot in those days. Maybe her mother liking poetry so much was part of why she had liked England and these old times.

Dot wondered if Aunt Tab had learned all this Wordsworth stuff in her guidebooks or maybe she'd learned it from school. That was one problem with her plan never to return to school—how would she learn stuff? She liked learning things. She wondered if she could do it all online. That would save her from having to cross any streets, and from having people say they were sorry for her or, even worse, saying that they knew how she felt.

"Did any Wordsworth teenagers run off and get pregnant? Were there suicides?" Dot asked, chewing a bite of her bacon sandwich, which wasn't half bad.

"No, not with these folks. Dorothy did get pretty depressed when her brother got married, but she rallied okay."

Dot was relieved. After those Marys, less drama seemed better. Things were tough enough as it was. That reminded her, "Aunt Tab, I saw a computer in the hall down by the reception desk. I'm going down to send a note to Junie."

"I'll just stay here and finish my tea. Oh, by the way, did I ever tell you that Dorothy Wordsworth was an orphan, too?"

• • •

Junie's email was waiting.

```
Dot, girl, you are ALL OVER THE PLACE!!!
Hiding ashes in restaurants—your aunt
sounds cool to me. And lost in the woods?
And meeting Jane Austen? That stuff never
happens to me! Whatever happened to the
nasty kids on the plane?

Tell me all the news.
BFF
```

Twenty-One: Less Drama Is Better

Dot liked that Junie sounded a little jealous.

Yo Junie,

The walk was really scary because I'd just been reading about Frankenstein's Monster who lurked in forests—when he got mad at people, he murdered them like swatting flies. It was written by my Mary Wollstonecraft's (how's that for a hard name to spell—it's hard to say out loud, too) nineteen-year-old daughter, also named Mary, when she ran away with her boyfriend, the famous poet Shelley who was rich and married to someone else at the time, but that didn't stop Mary from having babies with him.

Maybe everyone has a story like that and it just doesn't show when you see them in a store or something. Who knows what they've been through? Do I look different?

Weird that you ask about the nasty kid on the plane. It was really only one, a boy. His sister seemed OK. I can't believe it but I DID see him again—in a bookstore in London!! Yesterday! I turned around fast—don't think he remembers me—I'm just one of millions of people he's been mean to.

```
This place we're at now, Keswick in the
Lake District, is the Dorothy Wordsworth
place. Hardly any trucks—it's the nicest
place so far.

I still have my passport.
You better write back soon!
Your traveling friend,
Dorothy Mary-Jane
```

After sending it off, she googled the definition of estimable: "Deserving of esteem; admirable."

Twenty-Two: Aunt Tab Spouts Poetry

"First stop, Greta Hall. We're going to circle around Dorothy's houses today and then tomorrow we'll take a hike," Aunt Tab said, as she packed her daypack with an extra sweater. "They told me the weather around here changes fast, so take something warm."

"Who's Greta Hall?"

"It's Coleridge's house, and it's closest to here. Then Dove Cottage and then Rydal Mount. Those are Wordsworth houses. We'll have to take a bus for them."

Dot thought it odd that Coleridge, one of her mother's favorite poets, kept coming up. She thought of nasty Nick in the bookstore, reading a Coleridge book. And the way Dorothy Wordsworth had described him in the soup café, it sounded as he were some sort of political revolutionary.

Dot was starting to like her revolutionary lineage—Mary Wollstonecraft for sure, being all about women's rights back when they, *we*, she corrected herself, had none, and then her daughter Mary, and now Dorothy's friendship with Coleridge, who'd said the country's rulers, not the starving people, should be charged with treason.

Aunt and niece walked the couple blocks to Greta Hall. The streets were quiet and clean. Even though Dot stayed to the inside of the sidewalk, she wasn't gripped with the cold fear that she'd felt in London, and even in Alton. Except for the scolding lady at the Tourist Information Centre, everything about Keswick was pretty nice so far. She'd even managed

Twenty-Two: Aunt Tab Spouts Poetry

the bus stop business, and today it looked like more buses were in store for her.

Coleridge's house, sitting high on a hill up a gravel driveway, seemed too grand for how Dot thought a poet should live. It was two stories of creamy stucco, with lots of windows and an elegant rounded section on one side. "Dorothy found this house for Coleridge; she wanted to make sure they all lived close to each other. Let's knock on the door and see what happens," Aunt Tab said, reading her guidebook and stubbing her toe on a small step by the front door.

"You mean this isn't a museum, like Jane Austen's house?"

"Nope. Private home. But still," Aunt Tab said, knocking loudly.

"Well, don't leave any ashes here," Dot said. "That would be *so* wrong."

"Of course, Dot. I'm not a total twit."

They stood on the sun-warmed, pale stone that was the front stoop of Coleridge's house. Aunt Tab knocked again and they waited. But all was quiet in Coleridge's house.

"He's probably off visiting the Wordsworths anyway," Aunt Tab finally said and turned back toward the driveway. "Let's go. Coleridge walked, just like Dorothy, between here and her house, all sixteen miles, all the time, day or night. But we're taking the bus."

Dot was glad Aunt Tab hadn't bothered anyone. What would she have said? "Hello, we're here from America and we're wondering if Coleridge, that's right, the dead poet, is around? Is his friend, Miss Wordsworth, here by any chance? Oh, and William, too? What luck!"

Not!

Dot followed her down the hill toward the bus stop. Three people with a single soul, she quoted to herself. That's how Dorothy Wordsworth said Coleridge described her and her brother and himself. People thought a lot more about souls in those days; she could tell that from reading *Frankenstein* and now *Pride and Prejudice*. Back then, souls did things—they were the best and wisest part of each person, the part that knew what really mattered, and also the part you had to take the most care of because it lived forever.

Dot didn't know what she thought about the idea of forever. She didn't like the way forever was linked with the idea of heaven and hell. Her mother hadn't believed in heaven or hell—she said both places seemed too much like a cartoon where everything was either perfectly wonderful or completely horrible with no in-between at all. Even Dot was smart enough to be skeptical about anything so absolute. AT, for instance, wasn't turning out to be completely, absolutely terrible every single second, which was kind of a shock to realize.

Not that she was changing her mind about running away. If anything, she was more resolved, but now it seemed more like adventure than total desperation—the right thing to do instead of the only thing possible.

• • •

"If Dorothy Wordsworth was famous for anything, it was for knowing the hills and clouds and flowers around her so well that she became a part of them. And the same for the people she loved. Whatever her family and friends wanted, she'd do anything to make it happen. Her loyalty to her human and natural surroundings was so great that she wasn't important to herself, if you know what I mean."

Dot could tell Aunt Tab was trying hard to describe Dorothy Wordsworth, to make sure Dot understood.

"Mom and I loved to watch the clouds," said Dot, not even thinking, for once, about the careening red truck.

As they waited for the bus to Dove Cottage, the first Wordsworth house, Aunt Tab started spouting poetry. "And the whole daffodil poem, which is my favorite Wordsworth poem, was written from Dorothy's description of walking near their house, where we're going to be if this bus ever comes. I can't remember the whole thing, but here's a part." Aunt Tab cleared her throat, scraped her hair off her forehead and focused her eyes on a small, green park down the street:

Twenty-Two: Aunt Tab Spouts Poetry

"I wandered lonely as a cloud
That floats on high o'er vales and hills
When all at once I saw a crowd,
A host of golden daffodils;
Beside the lake, beneath the trees,
Fluttering and dancing in the breeze."

Aunt Tab stopped, harrumphed a little, and then hurried on. "And then it goes on about how the daffodils toss their heads gracefully and are more beautiful than the waves on the lake, and how when Wordsworth is feeling down, he remembers them,

And then my heart with pleasure fills,
And dances with the daffodils.

"In Dorothy's description of the real thing, which she wrote down in her journal, the daffodils weren't more graceful or more beautiful than the waves. It wasn't a competition. She said the flowers and the waves danced and laughed together. She was like that."

"Aunt Tab," said Dot, "I didn't know you knew poetry."

"We both did. Your grandfather taught both Thea and me to memorize lots of poems. He especially loved Coleridge—his poems are more mystical and have more ideas in them than Wordsworth's. People nowadays don't know what they're missing."

Twenty-Three: Two Months Ago Today

As the poetry ended, the bus arrived. It was a friendly blue and there were already some passengers on board. Aunt Tab said, "Good, traveling with the locals." Dot looked around as they found a seat and saw a few teenagers, some old people, and a housewife with a couple of small children. She gave the teenagers a hard second look. Nasty Nick wasn't among them.

Dot recited to herself, *"And then my heart with pleasure fills, and dances with the daffodils."* It would be nice to have a heart full of pleasure. She thought of the cheerful silken colors in *Dancing on the Edge*. Maybe it *was* possible to dance on an edge. Maybe edges weren't all bad.

Aunt Tab's voice brought her back. "Of course this bus wasn't here in Dorothy Wordsworth's day. As I said, she was quite a walker—rain or sun, daylight or moonlight; it was all beautiful to her."

Dot had never walked in the moonlight. She thought it sounded interesting, if you knew where you were and there weren't any Monsters or busy highways around.

"Why did Dorothy Wordsworth like Coleridge?"

"At first, everybody liked Coleridge. He told terrific stories and was handsome and enthusiastic. Lots of dark, curly hair. He loved to walk and he loved to play with words—both things Dorothy loved, too. Later, he got addicted to opium and it made him unreliable and Dorothy didn't like that. He invented the word 'psychosomatic' to describe how his mind and body were connected; he was either brilliant and strong or depressed and sick. Oops, here we are," Aunt Tab clattered off the bus, forgetting her bag.

Twenty-Three: Two Months Ago Today

Dot grabbed Aunt Tab's bag and hurried off the bus, not even thinking she might be carrying her mother's ashes. As they stood on the side of the road waiting to cross after the bus lumbered off, they looked around. There was a lake on one side, through some trees, and a small stone house on the other, with the sign "Dove Cottage." It was small, nothing like Coleridge's Greta Hall.

"Sounds very romantic and wonderful, but the Wordsworths didn't call it Dove Cottage. In their day it was Town End. Very different feeling," Aunt Tab observed, taking back her bag.

When they went inside, Dot didn't much like Dove Cottage or Town End or whatever you wanted to call it. It was dark and damp and chilly. The rooms were tiny, the ceilings low and the windows few. No wonder Dorothy preferred being outside. There was even an open stream running under the floor in one room—Dorothy had used it as a walk-in fridge, not that they had much food to keep cold. The kitchen was mostly just a big old wood stove, but a guide in the house said Dorothy made pretty good bread. She said that they always had company, so Dorothy had to do a lot of cooking, as well as tend the vegetable garden. The guide also said they ate a lot of oatmeal.

"Plain living, for sure," Aunt Tab said when they emerged from the house tour. "Their next house is supposed to be better—William had finally made a little money. We can walk there."

At first there was a sidewalk, and then a broad, open path, but after that, they came to nothing but the road's very narrow shoulder. The traffic on the road had built up quite a bit from the morning, and there were even a few trucks.

"I can't walk along that road, Aunt Tab."

They stood for a while at the end of the path, watching the traffic on the curving, two-lane road. "It doesn't get better. And we have to cross to the other side, too," said Aunt Tab, consulting her maps and peering ahead.

"Let's not," said Dot. The cold stony feeling she'd had outside the Seattle Library that horrible day settled on her brain as if it had never left, and would never leave again, gluing her feet to the ground and clouding her eyes. She started to shiver and couldn't get a good breath. She thought she might topple right over, smack into the traffic. Aunt Tab grabbed her in mid-tilt, and pulled her back into a brushy area away from the road.

"You're looking a mite pale," said Aunt Tab from a million miles away. "Let's sit here for a while."

So they did, and gradually Dot came back to normal, or whatever counted as normal in **AT**.

"It's two months ago today, that must be it," Aunt Tab murmured.

Twenty-Four: Feeling Safe

They took the bus back to Keswick with *two months ago today* repeating in an endless loop in Dot's head as she stared at her feet on the floor. Remembering and trying not to remember was taking up her entire attention. She felt like such a mess, such a baby. Her mother wouldn't like seeing her like this.

When they returned, Aunt Tab made Dot take two bites of a potato samosa at The Star of Alethea's pub. "I think a little hike," Aunt Tab finally said, looking up from her maps, which were spread all over the table, collecting crumbs and tea spatters. "Up here on Catbells," she pointed to a spot on the map, and then out the pub window to the roundish, brown peak on the other side of the lake. "Just to see, get some exercise, not to *do* anything." She looked at Dot to see if she'd understood.

Dot nodded.

After it was obvious that Dot wasn't going to eat anything more, Aunt Tab went to the girl at the reception desk to ask how to get across the lake to the bottom of Catbells. She said there was a small walk-on ferryboat that took hikers to different trailheads around the lake. The ferry dock was just down the street.

The wooden ferry, named *The Ancient Mariner*, bobbed in the light chop of the sparkly lake. Dot stood at the railing. She took a deep breath of the fresh water-scented air and felt a little better. She thought about Dorothy Wordsworth and the waves dancing with the daffodils. Other things danced in the wind, too. Kites, for instance. Once she and her mother had taken a ferry across Puget Sound to Bainbridge Island. It was a much

Twenty-Four: Feeling Safe

bigger ferry than this little Derwentwater one. On Bainbridge, they'd bought a kite in a hardware store; just a simple, diamond-shaped, paper one, orange and yellow with a round-eyed owl printed on it. On the return trip they flew it off the back of the ferry. About halfway across, sharp gusts of wind whipped it madly up and down and finally broke the string. They laughed as the kite caught one updraft after another, swooping happily with the seagulls, and then they waved it good-bye as, zoom, it plummeted into the cold, clear water. Holding hands, mother and daughter walked to the front of the boat and watched Seattle's skyscrapers gradually get larger, until they landed and took the bus home. It had been a fun day.

Dot didn't think this Keswick ferry was going fast enough to get a kite up in the air.

• • •

Aunt Tab and Dot disembarked on the other side of Derwentwater, the only passengers to get off at the small pier marking the trailhead to the top of Catbells. After more map-consultation, they set out, Aunt Tab loping along in the lead. It was a sunny afternoon and the path began fairly level, with trees on one side and fields on the other. Dot followed, trying to let the beauty of their surroundings soak in so much that there would be no space left for the thoughts and pictures that went with the phrase *two months ago today*.

"A kissing gate!" Aunt Tab laughed her barky laugh and stopped by a fence with a section that had a little enclosure with a swinging partition. "See. We have to go through it one by one, and the first person has to swing this little gate closed before the next person can go through. Cows and sheep can't figure it out."

Dot wished she could be as amused as Aunt Tab. If she'd felt better, she would have asked why "kissing."

After that, the path turned rocky and went more steeply up. The trees were replaced with bushes and boulders. They walked more slowly, and Aunt Tab stopped every now and then to exclaim over the increasingly lovely scenery around and beneath them. The higher they went, the more beautiful the views down to the lake and across the valleys to the surrounding peaks became. Even Dot noticed. The peaks around them weren't mountains like she was used to seeing, with crags and glaciers, but even so, these hills had a wild and challenging look when you got up close. Their path went near a few sheer cliff faces and they had to scramble over loose rock on some of the steep sections.

At the top, Aunt Tab and Dot toasted themselves with their one bottle of water as they admired the three-hundred-and-sixty-degree views. Brown hills with heathery lavender sides and green valleys, some with blue lakes at their bottoms, completely surrounded them.

Aunt Tab sighed. "Drink this in, Dot. There's nothing better."

Dot liked that she could see the horizon in every direction. No sudden surprises were possible. No Monsters, no trucks. Everything was out in the open; nothing could sneak up on you.

"Makes you realize how small you are," said Aunt Tab.

"That's not what I was thinking."

"What were you thinking, Miss Dot?"

"I was feeling safe."

"Hmm," said Aunt Tab. "Pass me the water. Let's sit here a while."

In the warmth and peace and quiet, they settled down by a row of large stones that marked the edge of the steep drop-off on the left side of their path. Dot started playing with the little rocks on the ground, stacking them one on top of the other and then watching them fall down. Aunt Tab just sat, not even pulling out her maps. She folded her hands in her lap and gazed quietly down the hillside to the lake below, where the little ferry boat was making feathery white patterns on its blue surface. Above them, pillowy clouds gathered and dissolved, like ghost lambs frisking and skittering across a huge pasture.

Into this stillness came the voices of two women. Dot looked around and could see no one. She looked at Aunt Tab, who'd closed her eyes and was now snoring lightly. Trying to spot the source of the voices, Dot finally noticed a path barely visible behind low-growing heathers and gorse, cut

Twenty-Four: Feeling Safe

into the side of the hill on the other side of the valley to their right. The voices of the women on the path traveled perfectly to where Dot sat.

Like at the Science Center at home, she thought. If you stand in a certain place you can hear people on the other side of the room as if they were right next to you. Her mother had taken her to the Science Center a lot; they both liked that you could handle and touch so many of the exhibits.

Dot sat up straighter and tried to follow the women's conversation.

Twenty-Five: Open Heart, Open Mind

"A good walk always calms my nerves," said one of the women hikers to the other. "I am delighted you accepted my invitation to visit."

Dot could just make out the speaker's long brown skirts and black shawl. Both women had stout walking sticks and were striding along at a good clip. Occasionally, one would stop and gesticulate with her stick, emphasizing her point.

"My dear brother, William, does much of his composing whilst we walk," the woman in brown went on. "He relies on me to take note of certain ephemera, such as the manner in which wind paints jagged patterns on the water or the way birdsong echoes, or how the evening light spreads its calm colors onto the highest rocks."

Dot could see that the speaker's companion was dressed in sky blue and maroon with a white cap. Her skirts ballooned out in front—she was obviously quite pregnant. "You are very poetical yourself, Miss Wordsworth. Do you write as much as your brother, or your friend Coleridge?"

"My, no! Just notes and phrases to remind us of what we have seen. I have no interest, frankly, to pen my nature to the page. My mind goes both too fast and too slow to be productive in that way. Believe me, I am of little use to anyone outside my small family."

"A loss to the world, Miss Wordsworth," said the pregnant woman, swatting at a bush with her stick.

Dot could see the woman in brown smooth her skirt as they walked. Even from this distance, she looked embarrassed, "Not at all, Miss Wollstonecraft. Please, let us change the subject."

Twenty-Five: Open Heart, Open Mind

It's Mary Wollstonecraft, thought Dot. And she must be pregnant with Mary Shelley.

"As you wish, Miss Wordsworth. I was about to comment on your beautiful and dramatic countryside," Miss Wollstonecraft said, sweeping both hands across the valley views. "The soul and the heart appreciate and understand this world far more intimately than does the head."

"Yes, I agree—the world often overwhelms my mind but delights my soul. William and I are convinced that the complexities of living are much smoothed by this nature around us. Rain and sun, dark and light—each so necessary to the life of the soul. We grow and blossom only by accepting it all."

Now it was Miss Wordsworth's turn to gesture toward the valley and the peaks on all sides. "To be able to cushion life's inevitable woe by living here, in this rooted and glorious place, is what keeps my heart in a safe home."

"I do not believe there is such a place for me," Miss Wollstonecraft admitted. "I am like the snail—the only home I truly know is my own skin. My constant experimenting has left me with many scars. My shell, sadly, is not even as protective a home as the snail enjoys. I have new hopes, though, now." She patted her abdomen.

"Coleridge is much like you," Miss Wordsworth said. "His dreams, Miss Wollstonecraft, are too big for our poor world."

"But you, Miss Wordsworth, are wiser than you know. I so long for the domestic peace you have constructed here." Miss Wollstonecraft stood still and spent a long time looking at the peaceful scenery, storing it up, maybe, for rough times ahead. Dot wondered what Miss Wollstonecraft's reaction would be if she were told that her unborn daughter Mary would grow up motherless, break up the marriage of a wealthy but politically radical poet, become a teenage runaway, marry him, and go on to write a famous story about an unhappy, murdering Monster. No fortune teller could ever make that up.

"And what of our young friend Miss Austen?" Miss Wollstonecraft broke their silence as they started walking again. "She has outdone us both.

The creature comforts of her life appear to far exceed anything you or I have. Yet they have not blindfolded her; she is clearly intelligent and perceptive."

"She spoke of writing novels, if I recall correctly," replied Miss Wordsworth. "Such fictions allow an author to make powerful observations in the guise of entertainment. Perhaps she will use that avenue to the advantage of the causes we both care so deeply about."

"I myself have used fiction to that end," said Miss Wollstonecraft. "I call my novel *Maria, or the Wrongs of Woman*. I fear, though, that it is too bleak to be entertaining."

"I would never try to write fiction. I have no power to create a world other than this beautiful one which surrounds me so overwhelmingly." Miss Wordsworth again gestured with her walking stick, and it caught the sunlight as she waved it toward Catbells' peak.

"Surely, it is not always so beautiful. There is struggle here, bad weather and great poverty, I believe. Yet I know that overcoming such challenges strengthens our belief in ourselves, and encourages us to attempt even more."

"Perhaps that is why William and I so love this craggy corner of England. Simple survival is indeed a physical challenge. On winter nights, I wear every stitch of clothing I own. For us, on cold, wet days, it is a battle won merely to get the fire going and the oatmeal boiling."

"Us? Does William assist in these household chores?" asked Miss Wollstonecraft, sounding surprised.

"No, not at all. His work is poetry only, and writing is very painful and time-consuming for him. But my neighbors and I help each other out, trading tea and flour, mutton and lettuce, help in the garden for help in the house. So many have so little."

"I see so many ways to make women's lives less painful and hopeless," said Miss Wollstonecraft. "I become impatient when I see how few understand the blatant unfairness of woman's position. With a few daring actions, the most beneficial changes could occur so quickly."

"I am less sure than you." Miss Wordsworth stopped walking and turned to her companion. "The problems of the world, including the ones

Twenty-Five: Open Heart, Open Mind

you speak of, seem to me impenetrable, like this sticker bush." She pointed to a patch of green near their path. "One person can do only so much. I am content to build a smaller life—and to know it, live it, and love it as deeply as possible. Even so, I must admit I am often at a loss. William's struggles to write a poem, for example, are agony to observe. Coleridge also suffers terribly. I can never do enough to help either of them. There is not a day long enough to make all the improvements needed in my small world, let alone the grand work that you propose."

Miss Wollstonecraft stretched her arms to the sky. "I so enjoy discussing these ideas with you. We women have sadly few chances for conversation that broadens our minds as well as expands our hearts. I firmly believe that an open heart requires an open mind. Men, I find, are more likely to use words for commerce or confusion than to advance the common good. And women's words! Far too often women's chatter accomplishes nothing beyond avoiding the imagined dangers of silence."

"There we are in complete agreement, Miss Wollstonecraft."

With that, the two women linked arms and began walking again. As they did so, they shaded their eyes and looked across the valley toward Catbells and the rocks on which she and Aunt Tab were leaning.

"Look there, Miss Wordsworth. There is another couple enjoying your beautiful and challenging countryside. Let us salute them as we round this bend in our path."

"I know most of the people in our district, but this distance is too far for my eyes to recognize them," said Miss Wordsworth. "Do you suppose their conversation is as thoughtful as ours?"

"As I have a tendency to overestimate people, I lean toward saying yes, which means likely the answer is no."

Miss Wordsworth laughed. "Now I see them better. Look at their attire! They look slight enough to be female, but they appear to be dressed in male garb."

"Indeed yes. I have thought before that britches or pantaloons of some sort would be more accommodating on long walks."

140

"If we are correct in thinking that they are women, we must commend their independent thinking," said Miss Wordsworth, adding, "I do not think William would approve."

"Perhaps Coleridge is more broad-minded?" Miss Wollstonecraft responded, saluting Dot and Aunt Tab with her walking stick.

The two women laughed and resumed their walk, soon reaching the bend on their path where they disappeared from Dot's sight and hearing.

Dot felt the warmth of the sun radiate into every part of her body, and with it, she felt the strong love and intelligence of Thea all around her. What a wonderful thing it was to be named after these three interesting women. "Thank you for bringing me here," Dot whispered to the air and to her still-sleeping aunt.

Suddenly, Dot heard another sound, this one rising quite harshly; very different from the conversational tones of Miss Wordsworth and Miss Wollstonecraft. Dot moved closer to the edge of the path and the drop-off below. Someone was yelling for help.

Twenty-Six: Dot to the Rescue

The yelling was repeated, and it was coming from far below. Forgetting about the ladies hiking in long skirts, Dot planted her feet and leaned carefully across the top of the stone barrier to peer down the steep side of the hill. She heard the yell again, from straight down and slightly to the right. She could see a pile of rocks and some stubby, green bushes. Amongst the brown and green she saw something bright red and what looked like sprawled arms and legs. Suddenly dizzy, she turned away quickly. "Down there!" she croaked at Aunt Tab, who'd snorted herself awake.

Aunt Tab hitched herself over to where Dot was leaning with her back against the rock. "It's okay. I'll look," she said, and wiped Dot's sweaty forehead with her sleeve.

Aunt Tab peered over the rock and saw what Dot had seen. Looking more closely, the patch of red moved, and soon resolved itself into a long-sleeved shirt or jacket and the person in it appeared to be trying to wave. Aunt Tab waved back, and yelled down, "Do you need help?"

"Help!" came wavering back up the hill.

"I'll go," Aunt Tab said, clambering over the stone barrier in a very awkward, old lady sort of way. She immediately lost her footing and fell, tearing holes in the knees of her pants.

Dot reached for Aunt Tab's disappearing shoulder. "You can't do that. I'll go."

Aunt Tab gratefully grasped Dot's hand and scrambled back to level ground. "Trails are one thing, downhill cross-country, something else entirely," she apologized. "And it's just a jacket—the red is just a jacket."

Twenty-Six: Dot to the Rescue

Dot gave her aunt a crooked grin and looked at the bright blue sky above her. Fortified, she scissored her legs over the stones and prepared to make a controlled slide down the hill. "Here, take the water." Aunt Tab tossed her the bottle as she dropped below the level of the path.

Dot's free hand grabbed at branches as she traversed across the face of the steepest parts, trying not to tumble down on top of whomever was at the bottom. About half-way down she stopped to catch her breath and map out her next steps. She felt brave and scared and daring and kind. She was going to *rescue* someone!

She noticed that her feet gripping crosswise on the steep slope were kicking down sheets of pebbly landslides. She hoped they wouldn't get bigger, like those helicopter snowboarders she once saw on TV, who skied right through their own avalanches as they zigzagged down vertical snowfields. It wouldn't be good to bury the person she was trying to save.

She could hear Aunt Tab shouting directions from above—"go right" or "go left"—but she ignored them because she was switching back and forth so much anyway, and she didn't know if Aunt Tab meant her own right or left, or Dot's.

Signaling to Aunt Tab that she was doing fine, Dot took careful aim at a spot near but not on top of the person below. The red splotch was now clearly and safely just a jacket. She couldn't make anything else out very well, blue jeans maybe, and possibly a green daypack off to one side. This was a game of Slip N'Slide in real life, she thought, as she got into the rhythm of moving her arms and legs from rock to branch to slippery foothold. A memory from a million years **BT** bubbled up—her mother laying out the plastic Slip N'Slide sheet and dousing Dot and Junie with the water hose, the water sparkling in the sunshine and cooling their summer-warmed skin. Not now, she said to herself. She didn't want to be distracted from the present.

She waved at the red splotch below and yelled, "I'm coming!" She wished she had a walking stick to wave and point like Miss Wordsworth and Miss Wollstonecraft.

A few marginally controlled slides later and Dot was at the level of the bushes just above where the person lay. She could now see him clearly, for it was definitely a boy. Not only that, it was definitely the only boy she knew in England and not only that, it was definitely the one boy she disliked the most in the whole world.

Twenty-Seven: Nick, Again

"I fell and broke my ankle," said Nick, his hair dirty and his face scratched. His blue eyes looked pained as he sat up and pointed to his left foot. He'd taken off his shoe and sock, and Dot could see that his ankle was grossly red and swollen. "I've been here flippin' forever. It hurts bad."

Dot turned to look at Aunt Tab, tiny and high up, and yelled, "Broken ankle!" pointing to Nick's foot. "Really hurts!" she added loudly.

"Remember me?" she said, looking at his face and ignoring the ankle.

"No," he looked at her impatiently. "We need to get out of here. This is only going to get worse and I can't walk on it at all. Is that water?"

"Here," she said, tossing him the water bottle. "You don't remember me at all?"

"Should I?" He sucked down about half the water. Dot realized he must have been here for a while. She had a candy bar in her pocket, but she decided to save it for later.

She sat back on her heels and watched him, not answering. He didn't look so nasty anymore—after all, he needed help, and she was all there was.

"How'd you get here?" she asked.

"Fell. I was reading," he said, pointing to a book in the dust a little way off, "and tripped on something. I was on that path up there." He pointed to a spot up and further along the path from where Aunt Tab was sitting.

"That's dumb," Dot said, scrambling over to retrieve the book. "Coleridge. The poet?"

Twenty-Seven: Nick, Again

"Yeah, he hiked on the most dangerous routes around here. Even today they say not to go the way he did."

"Sounds like good advice," Dot said, looking pointedly at Nick's useless ankle.

"Maybe. So why am I supposed to know you? And how do we get out of here?"

Dot looked up the raggedy hillside she'd just clambered down. She had no idea how they were going to get out of there. She certainly couldn't carry him.

"Is there another way to go that's not back up the hill?"

"Around there," Nick pointed past the bushes. "There's some uphill, but mostly it's a flat path that goes way around the lakeshore to Keswick. It's miles."

"Guess that's what we'll have to do," said Dot, feeling oddly energized.

"Maybe I can hop along if I lean on you," he said. "Is there a stick around that I could use?"

Dot walked back to the bushes, looking for a stick strong enough for Nick to lean on. There weren't any on the ground, and even if she'd had a knife, none of the branches were long enough to be of any use.

"Nope," she told him, not very disappointed. Even though she wanted to help, she had no intention of making this easy for him.

Meanwhile, Nick had scooted himself around to his daypack, his butt leaving a trail on the ground. He stuffed in Coleridge and the shoe he couldn't possibly have crammed onto his ballooning foot. He wrapped his sock around the bad ankle, tying it like a bandage.

"Bloody hell," he said, wincing as he did it. "Okay, you…what did you say your name was? Come over here now so I can try to stand up."

"I didn't say. It's Dot. You're Nick." She walked over to him, but very slowly. His choice of words just made her want to be even meaner. She knew it was wrong to be mean, but hey, she was going to help him out of the woods, so what did it matter how she did it? Anyway, he hadn't said thank you once.

"How do you know my name?'

"Tell ya later," she said, standing as tall as she could next to him, hoping he felt small and weak in comparison. She extended an arm toward him, and he grabbed it to steady himself while he hoisted himself upright on his good foot. He was balancing heavily on Dot.

"Put the water in your pack, and carry it on your good side," Dot ordered, figuring out the best way for them to proceed. Now that he was up, she had a better sense of how difficult this was going to be, and not just for him. Standing, it was clear that he was taller and heavier than she was, and it was going to be hard for her to stay steady against his unstable hopping.

While he adjusted the pack on his good side, Dot looked up at Aunt Tab, and pointed toward the bushes and the other path. "Going this way!" she yelled. She hoped Aunt Tab could figure out what she meant, and that her maps showed the other path, so she could get someone to come quickly from town to meet them. She doubted that she and Nick could make it for miles like this. Aunt Tab waved back, but didn't move from her rock.

They headed off awkwardly, Nick lurching against Dot before she expected it. He knocked her off balance almost immediately and they both fell into a tangled heap before they'd even reached the bushes.

"Let's try that again," Dot said as she got up first and planted her feet firmly so he could pull his way up. "You gotta tell me when you're going to hop like that."

"Maybe I can put a little weight on it," Nick said as he put his bad foot on the ground, and then yanked it up as if he'd touched a hot frying pan. "Bleeding hell. Guess not."

Dot shot him a freezing look, but tried to be more careful as they started off again. By the time they'd taken ten or fifteen steps and reached the bushes, they'd devised a rhythm of walking that enabled Dot to handle Nick's wobbling weight.

"So how do I know you?" Nick asked once they had gotten themselves established and didn't have to think through each move. "You said your name was Dot?"

Twenty-Seven: Nick, Again

"I met you and your sister on the plane."

Nick gave her a blank look.

He really doesn't remember how nasty he was about my mom, Dot thought. He must be cruel to so many people so much of the time that it all runs together. She thought about giving him a shove and watching him try to get up by himself. Eventually she'd help, but she'd watch him squirm around for a while first. Maybe later. For now, there was obviously no point in going into any more details about the airplane conversation, that's for sure. Just get him out of the woods and be done with him.

That got her thinking about being done with things. Her passport was still in her back pocket. She checked to make sure it hadn't become dislodged in all the hiking and sliding. Nope, still there. Did she still want to run away? Flying home early was making less and less sense—the trip was almost over anyway. That left staying in England. Until Nick came along, she'd been thinking she liked the Lake District better than the other two places. London was too big and noisy, and Alton hadn't raised her spirits like these hills and valleys and lakes had. This is the place she'd pick. But now it was contaminated—what if Nick lived here?

"You don't live around here, do you?" she said, trying to sound casual.

"No, in London. I like it here, though. The weather's not always so great, but that's what keeps it beautiful. Kinda like Seattle—I was just there," he added, sounding almost like a reasonable human being for the first time since she'd laid eyes on him.

"I like it here, too. My Aunt Tab and I are visiting. She's the person I was waving to."

"Will she send for help? Not that we're not doing too badly now, but we've a long way to go."

"Hope she did. Otherwise if I get too tired, I'll push you over and leave you here. Maybe I'll get someone to come back to get you, and maybe I won't."

"What's with you, Dot, or whatever you said your name was? What did I ever do to you?"

"That's for me to know and you to find out." Dot was enjoying this even though she knew she shouldn't. Her mother would be disappointed. Aunt Tab might even switch and take Nick's side.

They stopped talking because they'd reached the part in the path where there was an uphill grade and both had to concentrate on each step.

"Hopping uphill is harder," Nick admitted, as his hops got shorter and less steady. Finally he said they needed to rest for a few minutes. They both lowered themselves to the ground and had a drink of the water, which was now almost gone. Dot thought about her candy bar again, but decided to wait, in case they got lost and really desperate.

Who knows, maybe this would be her chance to walk in the moonlight, like Dorothy Wordsworth. She looked over at Nick, who was re-tying his sock bandage. This wasn't exactly what she'd had in mind, though. But then again, AT life in general wasn't exactly what she'd had in mind. That was such a pathetic understatement, she almost grinned, and she knew her mother would be.

Trees arched over the path where they sat, and Dot and Nick's attention was drawn to a couple of squirrels scampering up and down the tree trunks and out along the branches. They looked as if they were playing tag, taking turns being "it."

"My sister and I used to play tag all the time," Nick said. "You must know Nell. Is that how you know me?"

"I met Nell the same time I met you," Dot said.

"You're a flippin' mystery," Nick said. "I don't much like mysteries. Well, there's some I like. Coleridge is full of mysteries. Weird things happen in his poems all the time. And scary things, too." He started quoting,

"Like one who, on a lonely road,
Doth walk in fear and dread,
And, having once turned round, walks on,
And turns no more his head;
Because he knows a frightful fiend
Doth close behind him tread."

"It's scary that you can quote so much poetry."

Twenty-Seven: Nick, Again

Nick laughed. "It's from *The Rime of the Ancient Mariner.* One of Coleridge's most awesome. Awfully depressing stuff. People screw everything up."

"Reminds me of *Frankenstein.* All that hunting and chasing Victor did, looking for the Monster and making everything worse with his secrecy."

"You've read Mary Shelley's *Frankenstein?*"

"Yeah," said Dot, feeling proud, but not knowing quite why.

"Didn't think American kids did that sort of thing."

"Why not? We're not dumb, you know."

"No, but still, you're more into computers and film than literature. I know 'cause I was just there, in Seattle at a computer camp."

"You already said. I'm from Seattle."

"Is that where we met?"

"No! I already said." Dot was exasperated.

Dot rose and didn't help Nick get upright again. After he hitched himself up against a tree trunk, they set off along the path in their awkward hopping rhythm, not talking, hearing only bird sounds and the tiny scratchings of squirrels and field mice. Dot thought about Victor Frankenstein's Monster, and how Mary Shelley had seemed to suggest that if people had been nice to him from the beginning, none of the bad stuff, none the murders, might have happened at all. Of course, Victor's mother still would have died, because that was in the beginning of the book, before Victor had made the Monster.

Then she wondered if Victor would have been so driven to make the Monster, to create life from death, if his mother hadn't died. Dot could understand Victor's thinking—hadn't she felt it a million times, almost constantly, herself? But Mary Shelley, whose own mother died too, had written a story where that turned out to be a very bad idea because by wanting to make life, he'd made the Monster, who had caused a lot *more* death to happen.

All of this was complicated to think about while staggering along a dirt path, trying to avoid tree roots and being knocked against by a heavy person who was trying to balance on one foot while still making forward progress.

"Hope Aunt Tab has found some people to meet us pretty soon," Dot broke their silence and then stumbled on a rock.

"Should we rest again?" Nick asked. "This can't be easy for you either."

Big of him to notice. Maybe he was human after all.

"No, I'm fine," she said, squaring her shoulders and standing up straighter.

"Actually, I could do with a brief stop," Nick admitted.

"Then say so. Don't put it on me."

"Okay, you're right." Nick slid gratefully to the ground and Dot sat down too, not letting on how glad she was for the rest.

"So tell me again why you're here?" Nick asked, looking at his fingernails.

"I didn't say. It's kinda private."

"Oh, sorry. Don't mean to pry." He bent down and rubbed his ankle. "Ouch," he said.

"It looks pretty bad," Dot said. "Lots of colors. I think it's getting bigger, too."

"Yeah. I really need to get to a dispensary."

"A what?"

"A dispensary, a clinic, a doctor, you know."

"Oh. My Aunt Tab has been learning all these English words, but I haven't paid much attention. Guess I'll have to though, if I stay here."

"Stay here? You said you were just visiting."

Dot looked confused. She hadn't meant to say that. She patted her passport pocket again, and waited for the right response to come. When it didn't, Nick said, "There's your mystery self again. You know me but I don't know you. You're visiting but you're not. You're helping me but you don't want to. What's the deal, Dot? What did I ever do to you?"

"You were mean to me about my mom!" Dot burst out.

"What? I don't know you. Or your mother."

Twenty-Seven: Nick, Again

"You can't know her. She's dead. And you made a joke about her. On the plane. Last week. Coming here." Dot was crying now, and hated herself for doing so, but glad she was finally defending her mother against nasty Nick.

Nick stopped fiddling with his sock and rubbed his forehead. "Now I remember. You were sitting in our row. I was really tired, and didn't much want to come home. You were with that old lady. She gave me quite a talking to, I remember that. Can't remember exactly what I said, though. Sorry. Guess it was bad, huh?"

"Terrible, horrible, very bad, no good," sniffed Dot.

"Sorry," he said again. "Apology accepted?" He held out his hand to Dot.

"Not yet," she said. "Time to get going."

"Okay, have it your way," he shrugged, and hopped over to the middle of the path where Dot had stood back up. As they started moving again, she could tell he was trying not to lean on her quite so much.

They hopped and lurched their way along for another fifteen minutes not saying a word. Finally, Nick said, "Penny for your thoughts."

"What?" said Dot, startled. Thea used to say that to her, whenever Dot was quiet and not doing anything for a long time. She'd even give her a penny, too, when she told her what she'd been thinking.

"Nothing," answered Dot. "I'm not thinking about anything."

"Doubt it," responded Nick. "You look like the kind of girl who's always thinking."

"Well..." began Dot. Of course Nick was right, she had been thinking. One of the things she'd been thinking was that she really wanted to talk to a kid, and not a grown-up like Aunt Tab, about everything that was going on. Junie would be best, but maybe she'd have to make do.

"Well," she started again, "I was thinking about my mother and about ashes and about England."

"That clears things up just fine. Thanks so much," Nick said sarcastically.

"Hey, you asked."

"Yeah, I asked because I wanted to know. Not because I wanted to be riddled with riddles."

Dot slowed their pace a little. "I already told you my mom was dead, right? It only happened two months ago." Now she stopped completely, trying to get her voice under control. Nick waited, not saying anything and centering all his weight on his good foot.

When she could trust herself not to cry, she continued, "And Aunt Tab is taking care of me now, and she has some of Mom's ashes and we're leaving them places. Places that meant a lot to my mom, although I didn't know it before. Places about who I was named after."

"Slow down there, Dot, you're losing me again. I get it about the mother and the aunt and the ashes. But what about the places and the names?" Nick sounded genuinely interested, not mocking at all.

As Dot was gearing up to explain, they both heard voices and footsteps in front of them. "They should be along this path somewhere." It was Aunt Tab and from the tromping behind her, it sounded as if she were leading an entire troop of Boy Scouts.

Less than a minute later, they came into view. Aunt Tab had not only found a troop of Keswick Boy Scouts, she'd found herself a stout walking stick, too.

"There you are! Goodness, Dot, what a hero you are. This boy's foot looks terrible. Scouts, do your duty!" Aunt Tab loosed the Boy Scouts on Nick and they swarmed around him, opening a canvas stretcher and splinting his ankle amid shouts of "This way! No, this is the way it goes! No, *I* got the badge. Do it like *this*."

Aunt Tab gave Dot a big hug and rubbed her thumb across a tear track on Dot's dusty cheek. She took a longer look at Nick, and said, "Say, isn't that the nasty boy from the airplane? Has he been on about Thea again? I'll break his other ankle," and she stalked over to the stretcher.

"No, stop, it's okay, Aunt Tab," said Dot, running over to get between Nick and Aunt Tab.

"Aunt Tab, this is Nick. Nick, this is my Aunt Tab," she introduced them, thinking her mother would be proud of her for performing such civilities.

Twenty-Seven: Nick, Again

"Well, humph, young man, I do hope you've learned some manners since we met last," said Aunt Tab, not offering to shake hands.

"Hello," said Nick weakly, more focused on what the Boy Scouts might be doing to his ankle. "Stop it, that bloody hurts," he yelled at them.

"Maybe we should just head on back to Keswick. Nick has to go to the dispensary," Dot said. "Great stick you found, Aunt Tab."

Twenty-Eight: Dear Mom

Back at The Star of Alethea, Aunt Tab and Dot had a late afternoon tea and talked over their day's adventures.

"Can't believe that nasty Nick turned up again. Here of all places," Aunt Tab said between big bites of a ham and cheese sandwich.

"Remember when we saw him with his sister in the airport?" Dot asked, trying something called Gentleman's Relish on a cracker. It was spicy and dark, a little like chutney, but not so sweet. She liked it.

"No. Were they ordering people around?"

"Not exactly. They looked sad. I think their parents were supposed to pick them up and they hadn't come. Nell was crying a little, and I overheard Nick saying something that made me think their parents forget about them a lot."

"I do remember now. Takes awful parents to raise such a rude boy. Just as well he broke his ankle. Those Boy Scouts seemed to think it was a bad break."

"Aunt Tab, now you're being mean."

"Just thinking, that's all. Good people die. Bad ones live."

"Don't talk like that," Dot said. Aunt Tab was irritating sometimes. Just blurting out whatever you're thinking isn't always good for the people within hearing range. Even true things can be said in lots of different ways. Dot was surprised that she was thinking like this, and wondered if it had to do with being in England and having overheard all the thoughtful conversations of Miss Wordsworth, Miss Wollstonecraft, and Miss Austen. She decided she preferred the formality of the "Miss" instead

157

Twenty-Eight: Dear Mom

of calling them by their first names. It was more respectful and honoring. She wondered if Junie would agree, and wondered when she'd next be able to talk to her. Depended on what she did with that passport in her pocket. And if she could solve the no-money problem.

Aunt Tab quieted down, except for chewing and swallowing. Dot ate a few more crackers and decided she wouldn't tell Aunt Tab that Nick had told her where he was staying, and had invited her to visit once he'd gotten his ankle splinted and some pain medicine in him. He was at a small apartment, he called it a flat, that friends of his parents owned, in an old house on a street just a couple over from The Star of Alethea. She hadn't promised, but she'd said maybe she'd come.

"We'll do another hike tomorrow," Aunt Tab finally broke their silence. Gulping her second cup of tea, she went on, "The ashes, you know. Dorothy comes first in your name and makes the perfect end to our mission. I was thinking we'd hike back up to the top of Catbells. What do you think?"

"About what?" Dot hadn't been listening.

"Your mother's ashes. Dorothy Wordsworth. Catbells. Aren't you listening?"

"No. I'm going upstairs." Aunt Tab was getting too bossy and she needed a break.

• • •

Back in their room, Dot pulled out the pad of paper she'd brought and found a pen in a drawer.

Dear Mom,

I don't know where you are, but I'm in Keswick, right near Dorothy Wordsworth. I've been learning a lot about the women you admired so much that you named me after them. Dorothy Wordsworth, Mary Wollstonecraft, Jane Austen. I wish I had paid more attention when you told me about them, but I didn't. You left me some hints on *Dancing on the Edge*, didn't you?

Anyway, I like all three of them. You might not believe this but I've met them all. They've been getting to know each other, too. Miss Austen helped me when I got lost walking to Cassandra's Cup. She was very nice. She's the youngest one, and I guess the most famous, but the other two are pretty great, too. I'm reading *Pride and Prejudice* but I don't like how the mother is so silly.

I'm still figuring out why you made Dorothy Wordsworth my first name. I think it has something to do with how she's the superglue that holds everyone together. She seems to care more about other people than she does for herself. She's a friend of Coleridge's, one of your favorite poets. And she really loves nature.

I like Miss Wollstonecraft, too, but she's kinda scary. Very sure of herself and very mad when things aren't fair. She's pretty emotional, too—jumping off bridges and all that. Maybe she's one of

Twenty-Eight: Dear Mom

those pioneer people who think so far ahead of their time that nothing works out for them even though they are right all along. I read her daughter's book, *Frankenstein*. Her name was Mary, too. She ran away and married Shelley, another one of your favorite poets.

Now I'm trying to decide what to do next. Should I run away and stay in England? Or should I go home? I guess Aunt Tab will move into our house. I don't love the idea. She's NOT YOU! But I think she's trying. Maybe I should too.

I do know that I like the Lake District a lot. You must have, too, even though you never saw it. It's beautiful—hills and valleys and lakes, lots of green and blue. Aunt Tab and I took a little ferry and went on a hike this morning. I met a boy who broke his ankle and I helped him out of the woods. It was hard. At first I didn't want to help him, but then I did.

Maybe you already know all this. Sometimes I think you're right here and already know everything.

I love you so much, Mom, and even if you are right here, it's not the same at all. I miss you and miss you *and miss you. I will always be looking for you. I hope someday I'll see you.*

Forever yours, yours forever,
Your daughter,
Dorothy Mary-Jane

Dot blotted a few tear spots off the paper, and then folded it three times and put it in her back pocket with her passport. She combed her hair with her fingers, grabbed her jacket and went down the stairs, through the swinging doors and into the lobby, avoiding Aunt Tab who was still chowing down in the dining room.

She was going to cross a street by herself for the first time **AT**.

Twenty-Nine: The Tarot Speaks

Unfortunately for Dot, the way to Nick's was not through the pedestrian-friendly, no-traffic part of Keswick. Fortunately, though, she was facing oncoming traffic, so she had plenty of time to duck inside a store or flatten herself against a wall to avoid things like huge red trucks. Plus, there was only one main intersection she had to cross.

Even so, she felt like a small, defenseless crab abandoned by the tide, eyes swiveling like mad, scuttling every which way to avoid careless runners and swooping sea gulls. She paid attention, though, and focused on what was really out there, and not on what was in her mind. Nobody could possibly appreciate the difficulty of what she was doing, but she remembered something Miss Wollstonecraft had said about the pleasures of succeeding at physical challenges. Surely this scary walk along the street counted. It was exhausting, worse than rescuing Nick, and she was only halfway there.

No. 12 Derwent Street, Nick's apartment, was now across an intersection and halfway down the next block. Crossing the street was the biggest obstacle. She stopped and stood well back from the curb, forcing herself to watch for a while. When some other people came along, she held her breath and scooted across the street with them.

Only when she was safely on the inside of the sidewalk on the other side did she let out her breath. She wanted to thank the people she'd tagged onto, but they were already on their way—they'd never know what a favor they'd done. Seems like that happens a lot, Dot thought, people helping or

Twenty-Nine: The Tarot Speaks

hurting each other and never knowing it. More stuff she wished she had a friend to talk to about.

She arrived at Nick's blue-painted door and, feeling brave from her walk, knocked loudly. Nick opened a window from a second floor above the door and shouted down, "It's open. Come on up." She pushed open the door and went up a narrow, wooden staircase. Nick was sitting by a window overlooking the street. He was leaning sideways in a cushioned chair with his bad foot on a stool. A little dust from the trail still clung to his curls, but his face looked pretty well scrubbed. Maybe the nurses at the dispensary had cleaned him up.

Dot looked around the room, which was small with striped wallpaper and white trim. One wall was covered with books behind floor-to-ceiling, glass-fronted bookshelves. There was a brightly colored Persian rug on the floor.

"Thanks again for rescuing me," he said. "I called Nell, and she says hi. She remembers you, and she remembers how awful I was. Sorry."

"That's okay," said Dot, standing in the middle of the room and not being sure why she'd come, or if it was a good idea.

"There's soda in the fridge if you want some."

"No thanks. My mom and I don't drink soda. We call it pop in Seattle."

"Sorry about your mum."

"Yeah."

"My mum's alive but we don't see her much. I don't think she really likes us. It's not the same thing as being dead, I guess, but…"

"No," said Dot. She couldn't imagine what it would be like to have a mother who didn't like you.

They didn't say anything for a while, and then Nick said, "Would you get me a soda, a pop? I'm supposed to keep this up as much as possible," he pointed to his ankle, now thickly encased in a navy blue splint with Velcro straps banded all across it.

"Sure," said Dot, as Nick added, "The kitchen's off the right, down that hall."

Dot returned with an orange soda in a bottle and handed it to Nick.

"It needs an opener," he said, laughing, "You really don't drink this stuff, do you?"

"No. I'll get it. Where is it?"

She returned with the opener and Nick drank some of the soda, and then put the bottle on the floor by his chair. He asked her what she was doing in Keswick, and repeated what he'd said on the trail about wanting to hear her story about the names and places.

"It's long," Dot stalled, but realized she wanted to tell him. She sat down cross-legged on a blue-and-yellow rug by one of the bookcases. It wasn't Tinkerbell, but it had her same colors. And the books at her back were comforting. She began with the places and the ash. She wasn't ready to talk about how her mother had died, and she hoped Nick wouldn't ask.

"How did she die?" Nick interrupted.

"Truck." The words just came out. "She got hit by a truck on the street. She wasn't on the street. We were on the sidewalk, waiting to cross."

"Wicked," said Nick. "Did you see it?"

Dot nodded, no longer able to speak as the pictures rushed across her unwilling eyes.

Nick watched her and then said, "Sorry, I shouldn't have asked."

"It's okay," Dot said, wiping her face on her jacket sleeve. "Anyway, Aunt Tab's taking care of me now, I guess. There's no one else. And she brought me to England because of my names and to leave my mom's ashes in places."

"What names?"

"My real name is Dorothy Mary-Jane. It turns out I'm named after Dorothy Wordsworth, Mary Wollstonecraft and Jane Austen."

"Bloody hell, that's terrific." Nick was clearly impressed.

"Why? Do you know them?" Dot was getting used to English swear words.

"Who doesn't?"

"Well, I didn't. But now I do, a little. I think I've met them," she added.

Twenty-Nine: The Tarot Speaks

Nick didn't pick up on this. "So how long are you here in Keswick? You've seen all the Wordsworth places? And Coleridge?"

"Some. We're here tomorrow and then we leave." She didn't mention about running away and staying in England. "Aunt Tab and I need to leave some ash in a Dorothy Wordsworth place."

"How about on her grave? She's in St. Oswald's churchyard at Grasmere, just down the road. Ancient stone church, grassy cemetery, flowering bushes. Just the thing."

"Maybe. Mom might like that. No big roads around?"

"No, Grasmere's smaller than Keswick. And the cemetery's out behind the church, away from the road. The River Rothay runs along the far end of the cemetery, near all the Wordsworth graves."

"Sounds nice. I'll tell Aunt Tab."

"They say I should try to walk a bit tomorrow. I'll come with you, if you like."

"To make up for being so mean?" Dot said, knowing she sounded rude. Maybe some of Aunt Tab's blurting-things-out habit was rubbing off on her.

Nick looked a little startled. "You Americans," he said.

"I don't know what I am. I don't really have a home anymore. I'm thinking about running away." Dot wasn't sure why she'd told him.

"I think about running away a lot. Sounds like you have, had, a really good mother, but I don't, particularly. If you did run away, where'd you go? I'd go to Italy. Want to come?" Nick asked as if it were a perfectly reasonable next step.

The suddenness of this move from an idea to a plan took Dot by surprise. "I don't know. I was kinda thinking maybe I'd just stay in England because of how my mom liked it so much—I didn't even know that before. And she never got to come."

"Tell you what. I'll do your tarot and maybe that will help us decide." Nick reached around for a deck of large cards on the window sill behind him. "Do you know tarot cards? They don't tell the future but they can help make decisions," he said, holding the deck out to Dot.

"No. My mom didn't go for that stuff." But she got up from the rug and took the cards from Nick. Shuffling through them, she said, "This is weird. I had a dream about cards like these. It was since I've been here, too, not in Keswick, but in London. My three ladies were playing cards, in my dream, I mean, and talking and pointing at them. They were laid out in a kind of cross pattern, all different colors with pictures like these."

"Awesome," said Nick. "They were shaping a life story. Maybe yours. What did they say?"

"I couldn't catch any of their words." She paused and looked over at Nick, "Hey, this is all make-believe anyway, isn't it?"

"Hard to say. Stranger things have happened. Here, let's do you."

Nick told her to shuffle the cards and then give them back to him. He lifted his leg and moved it to the edge of the stool so there was room for him to lay out ten cards, five in a cross, with one more lying crosswise on the middle card, and then four in a vertical row to the right of the cross. They were all face down, except for the one on the bottom in the middle of the cross.

He took that card out from under the other one and showed it to Dot. It was a brightly colored drawing of a person in starry clothing with wide, sweeping sleeves and cuffed boots. The person was standing on the edge of a precipice and stretching his (or her, the drawing could be either) arms out to a warm, yellow sky. A cheerful sun shone down from the right top corner and a friendly little dog barked at his or her feet. He or she balanced a pole with a bandana tied to one end over one shoulder and held a white rose in the other hand. In the background was a stormy sea, or possibly a snowy mountain range. The picture looked familiar to Dot. Underneath the picture were the words, "The Fool."

"This is awesome!" said Nick. "This represents you. Don't worry, Dot, The Fool doesn't mean stupid. It's a card for possibilities, for the beginning of exciting times. This is perfect! Might even be Italy in the background, there."

"I'm not sure I like excitement anymore," Dot said, beginning to long for Tinkerbell, spread out on top of her bed back at The Star of

Twenty-Nine: The Tarot Speaks

Alethea. The precipice in the picture looked more dangerous than a sidewalk curb, and she was worried that The Fool might step right off by accident. She remembered what the card reminded her of—this was the figure she had seen in the curling smoke rising from the chimney near Miss Austen's house.

"No, I mean good excitement," he amended. "And it's not necessarily excitement in an all-jazzed-up way. It means beginnings and decisions, things like that. Don't worry." He stopped to look at her, worried. "We don't have to do this. I just thought it might help you make up your mind about running away. And then when you said your ladies had them..."

"Okay, do one more."

Nick picked up the card that was on top of The Fool. "This card shows the situation you're asking about." He turned it over. Dot saw a picture of a woman and six swords on a boat being taken across the water by a ferryman. "Cool," said Nick. "This is about taking a trip, and it shows you have a helpful partner."

"I hope not Aunt Tab. Could be my three ladies?"

"Could be me," Nick said. "Let's keep going. Those four cards that make the cross have to do with the recent past, the immediate future, and your head, and your heart." He turned them over all at once. Three of the cards showed sad or dissatisfied people, and only one had a happy scene.

Dot listened while Nick explained that the four cards all agreed that she'd had a very sad thing happen to her recently and that she was uncertain about what to do next. "Can't argue with that," Dot said, looking carefully at each. One card showed a person sitting up in bed with her hands over her face, as if she'd just woken from a terrible nightmare. Dot could almost see the person shaking. Another card showed three swords piercing a bleeding heart. Nick said it wasn't real blood—it usually meant that some angry words needed to be spoken, or recently had been spoken.

"What about this one? It looks the happiest." Dot was glad to turn to a card with a rainbow of cups arching over a happy couple and two little children dancing by their sides with a pretty landscape of a river, trees, grass, and a storybook cottage in the background. It reminded her of the woods near where she'd met Miss Austen, only on a nice summer day.

"Yeah, hard to miss that one. And it's in a great position for you, too. It has to do with having a happy family, obviously, and it has to do with your immediate future. It's a family, or a group of good friends that you have, or will have."

"Does it tell me where?"

"Nada."

"At least it's not bad," Dot said, looking back at the gloomy, bleeding heart picture.

Next Nick turned over the four cards in the vertical line, starting at the bottom. "Ah, The Hermit. I like this one; it's saying you need a guide to answer your question. See, he's carrying a lantern and he's out studying the world. He's a very good person to take advice from. Could be me," he said, handing her the card.

"Doesn't look like you," she laughed and handed it back to him. "See the white beard?"

"It could happen," he said, replacing the card on the stool and stroking his hairless chin.

The card above The Hermit was another happy-looking one. The picture was crowded with a castle, more dancing people, four sticks in the ground holding up garlands of flowers, and two other people holding up more flowers. All of the happy cards had lots of yellow on them.

"This is very good, Dot," Nick said. "This is where you are right now, and it shows a good foundation. Whatever you are building, whatever you're thinking, it's solid and strong. Lots of potential."

Dot felt good, and then immediately felt silly. After all, these were just a bunch of pictures on a deck of cards.

The next card up was another worrisome one. It was unnerving how the pictures could flip-flop her emotions so powerfully, zinging her between happy and worried. This latest card showed two people in rags, one hobbling on crutches, in a snowstorm on a black night outside a church. Behind them, a colorful stained-glass window shone through the falling snow.

Twenty-Nine: The Tarot Speaks

"This is another one about loss, obviously, but see the window. It's like there's been a physical loss, but the spiritual side is still shining," Nick said, pointing at the beautiful church window, bright against the darkness around it.

"I don't want to be told I'm stumbling though the snow in rags. Is that you staggering on the crutches next to me?"

Now it was Nick's turn to laugh. "Well, at least you have company." He flipped the card across his hand back onto the foot stool. "It might be saying that the people around you don't have a clue about you. They pity you for being out in the snow in rags, but really you're strong and bright inside."

"Sometimes I think Aunt Tab gets me and sometimes she doesn't."

"Mothers…grown-ups, don't realize how important they are to kids," Nick said, looking nowhere in particular. He kicked his good foot and knocked over his empty pop bottle.

Dot leaned over to pick up the bottle and thought maybe Nick wasn't talking about the same thing she was talking about. But she didn't know how to go on, so she went back to the cards.

"This tarot story reminds me of those drawing games with numbered dots all over the page that look like nothing, but if you draw a line between consecutive numbers, you end up with a picture. Dot to Dot, they were called. Did you have them when you were little?"

"Yeah. Nell and I used to have races with them. I always liked shouting out what the picture was after connecting the fewest number of dots."

"My mom used to say it wasn't so much about the main picture, but about how many other things you could make if you connected every second dot or made your own fraction dots in between. You could make dozens of pictures, all different."

"Your mum sounds cool."

"Yeah."

Dot suddenly needed to change the subject. "So, will the last card tell me what to do?"

"Sort of. Let's see…" and he turned it over. It was a picture of a person looking up at a big, gray, cumulous cloud and cradling seven cups, each holding something different—jewels or garlands or snakes or castles or devils and also something covered up. "Whoa, not much help here."

"Why," asked Dot. "What does it say?"

"Sorry, Dot, it just says you have a decision to make, and you don't know what to choose."

"Great. Thanks a lot, tarot cards."

"But don't give up. That's part of what this card is saying. It's also warning you to watch out because some of the choices aren't as good as they may look. Mainly, it's saying you're in charge. You get to make the decision. You might wish you didn't have to, but you do, and you have the smarts to make the right one. You just have to take your time and think about it."

"Oh," said Dot, remembering that the ladies had been talking all week about how important it was to make up your own mind and then live by your choices.

"So, what do you think? Italy?" he smiled as he gathered up the tarot cards. "I've got plenty of money for the tickets and everything."

Dot looked at him and then smiled. "I'll think about it, and tell you later."

Thirty: Wishes to Ashes

"Would you help me with something, Nick?" Dot said, as Nick put the tarot cards back on the window sill.

"Of course. You practically saved my life, remember?"

She took the letter to her mother out of her pocket and unfolded it, carefully smoothing the three folds. "This is a letter to my mother. I want to burn it and put the ashes with her ashes—" Dot's voice faded as a picture of ashes welled up and she had to stop until she could sound normal again. "Anyway, you know what I mean. So do you have any matches? And something to keep the ashes in?"

"By the fireplace in the next room. You could burn it on the hearth there. And I think there's a sandwich bag in the kitchen. Would you like company? I'm not supposed to get up, but this is important. I'll help if you want."

Dot didn't answer, but went into the kitchen to find the bag. When she came back, she said, "No, I think I'll do it by myself." She walked into the next room, adding, "Thanks for offering, though."

The fireplace was in the center of the wall opposite the doorway. The mantle was painted white and the hearth was set with chipped, blue-and-white tiles painted with pictures of flowers and rabbits. Dot thought her mother would like it. She knelt on the floor in front of the hearth and set the plastic bag, the letter, and the matches each on its own tile in a row in front of her knees.

Dot reread the letter, slowly whispering each word. Every syllable came from deep inside her, coursing strongly through her whole body before escaping lightly into the air. It took a while to get through it.

Thirty: Wishes to Ashes

"Yell if you need anything," Nick shouted from his chair in the other room.

When she'd finished whispering the letter, Dot laid the paper gently on the tiles and struck a match. She held the match above the page, unable to decide where to set it alight—on which corner, at the top or the bottom? As she hesitated, the match burned to her fingers. "Ouch," she said and dropped it right in the middle. The flame caught on the paper below and burned evenly outward from the middle to each edge.

It was over very quickly. The burned page was now flakes of charred paper, most tiny but one piece from the bottom of the page was large and intact enough so that a faint shadow of five words was visible: "I think you're right here." The ash was so fragile that Dot wasn't sure how she could pick it up and put it into the bag. She wished she'd thought of that ahead of time, and put the paper on a plate or something. Too late for that, though, so as carefully as a mother kitten moving her new babies, she gently reached and scooped and dusted as much ash as she could into the bag. She couldn't quite get it all, but it would have to do.

Rising from the hearth, she folded the bag down tight and small and slid it down deep in a front pocket of her jeans.

Thirty-One: Third and Last

"Aunt Tab, I have a suggestion about where to scatter Mom's last ash."

"Dot, where have you been? I looked all over this place for you."

"I went out."

Aunt Tab's face lost its irritated expression, and she moved toward Dot like she wanted to give her a congratulatory hug, but Dot slipped to the side. Aunt Tab's hugs made her feel small.

"Okay, then, what's the suggestion?" Aunt Tab picked a bit of lint off her sweater to cover for the non-hugging.

"Dorothy Wordsworth's grave in Grasmere."

"Been doing your homework, I see. Tell me why you think that's a good place."

"It's in an old churchyard, away from a road. It's quiet and there's nice trees and bushes around. And she's there with her whole family, all together."

"Sounds peaceful and lovely. Perfect, in fact. Good job, Dot. Where did you get the idea?"

"Actually, it was Nick's idea." Dot wasn't sure, but she thought she might be blushing.

"Nick! That nasty boy who got his comeuppance on the path this morning? Good grief, girl, what has come over you that you would take advice from someone like that?"

"You said yourself it was a good idea, Aunt Tab."

"Well, yes, but I hate to think of him being involved in it."

Thirty-One: Third and Last

"Actually, I invited him to come with us," Dot said, realizing that wasn't strictly true, as Nick had invited himself.

"Well, double good grief, that's all I have to say," Aunt Tab said. She was shaking her head but Dot thought she could see a little smile hovering in her eyes. "And have you and Nick decided when we shall go and execute on his excellent suggestion?"

"Tomorrow morning in the early light. We can take the same bus we took to Dorothy's house yesterday."

"Well, well," said Aunt Tab, smacking her lips in a satisfied way. "Will wonders never cease? Thea is loving this, I hope you know."

• • •

Next morning, Dot and Aunt Tab woke early, rising with the sun. The few clouds outside their window were simple cirrus, holding no threat of rain. Aunt Tab dressed quickly, saying she wanted to eat her share of the Full English Breakfast before they left.

"I'll be down in a few minutes," said Dot, standing at the window and watching the sun wash down the heathery sides of Catbells.

"Bring your jacket when you come and we'll leave for the bus stop right from there." Aunt Tab banged the door shut behind her.

So this was it. The last ash drop. The last good-bye. What next? Outside, the sun had reached the bottom of the valley and was already skipping across the lake, streaking Derwentwater's blue surface with white and gold. It was so beautiful—she wanted to walk every walk that Dorothy Wordsworth had ever walked, to see every view she'd ever seen. She wanted to explore. She wanted to be daring. She wanted to make things happen. She wanted Miss Wordsworth, Miss Wollstonecraft, and Miss Austen to be proud of her. Mostly, she wanted her mother to know she was figuring things out.

Finally, she turned away from the window and looked around the hotel room. Tinkerbell lay on top of her white duvet cover, looking like a giant tarot card picture. Dot walked over to her bed and lay down on Tink, head to head. Tinkerbell gave her no advice. It really was up to her. She rose, found her jacket, and went downstairs to meet Aunt Tab.

• • •

Nick was already at the bus stop, his left foot encased in its blue splint. He splashed a happy grin in Dot's direction, and then very politely shook hands with Aunt Tab. She, only slightly less politely, shook hands back.

"I'm honored to be a part of this ceremony," he said.

"Harrumph," said Aunt Tab.

Despite Nick's smile, or maybe because of it, Dot felt awkward, too, and was glad when the bus came. The bus driver helped Nick get up the steps and he sat in a seat opposite Dot and Aunt Tab, stretching his injured leg across the seat.

The bus bounced down the same road they had taken when they'd visited Dove Cottage the morning before. They'd ridden through the edge of Grasmere then, but Dot and Aunt Tab hadn't realized it. Now they got off at the stop the bus driver said was closest to St. Oswald's church, where the Wordsworths were buried. "Down this road here, and then to the left," he said after helping Nick negotiate the steps again.

The three walked slowly down the street, passing small souvenir and clothing stores just opening up. Dot stayed on the inside of the sidewalk and Aunt Tab was in the middle. They walked slowly to accommodate Nick's limping gait.

"Look at all this useless stuff," Aunt Tab griped, "expensive things that people can't help buying just because they're on vacation."

"The most famous shop here sells gingerbread," said Nick, pointing down the street. "It's right across from the church."

"Can't be as good as my mom's," Dot said. It was getting a little easier to talk about Thea, to make her part of the conversation and not have the worst of the memory pictures whoosh down on her, sucking away all the air and turning everything red.

Thirty-One: Third and Last

"Dorothy Wordsworth loved it," Nick said. "If it's open when we get there, I'll buy you some and you can taste for yourself."

The shop was open, and clearly aimed at the tourist trade, as Aunt Tab wasted no time in pointing out. A sign outside explained that this small, whitewashed-stone building had been built in the 1600s as a school. Inside, the tiny space was crammed with shelves and counters, which were themselves crammed with jars and bottles of rum butter, toffee sauce, and fruit jams. All around were stacks of gingerbread wrapped in white paper with a blue label.

A woman with a cheerful smile and a white apron sold them gingerbread and gave them a small piece of fudge "since you're our first customers of the day." Aunt Tab put the fudge in her bag and Dot carried the gingerbread. "Let's eat it in the cemetery," she said, "after the ash."

As Nick had said, the entrance to St. Oswald's churchyard was right across the road from the gingerbread shop. They walked on a grass path around the unpretentious stone building to the gravestones in the back. No one was there.

Dot wandered among the stones, looking at the names and the dates from one hundred, two hundred, even three hundred years ago. The grass in between the stones was dotted with tiny daisies. At first Dot tried to avoid stepping on them, but there were too many. When she looked behind her, she saw the flowers spring back up, none the worse after her step. She walked down to the river bank. The river was small, much smaller than the Thames had been in London, but larger than the creek in the woods where she'd been lost outside of Alton. She liked that there was water in all three places. There'd been a lot of water on the tarot cards, too, rivers and oceans, rain and snow.

"Here she is," called out Aunt Tab, standing by a gravestone. "They're all here: Dorothy, William and his wife Mary (yet another Mary, but no relation to the Wollstonecraft Marys), their children, and Dorothy's other brother John."

Dot walked back from the river bank and Nick came over from where he'd been looking at some different gravestones. "The Nelsons are over there," he said, "Sarah Nelson is the one who started the gingerbread business."

They gathered around the Wordsworth family, Nick slightly off to one side. The Wordsworth gravestones were upright gray tablets, very plain with angled tops and spots of white and green lichen growing all over them. They were very close together. Dorothy's said only "Dorothy Wordsworth 1855."

Dot felt a little self-conscious. It wasn't scary, like in London, or funny, like at Cassandra's Cup. This was the last one—she felt solemn.

"Aunt Tab, can I do it this time?" She put the gingerbread on the grass behind her and reached into her pocket for the bag holding the ash of her letter.

"Your mother will be honored." Aunt Tab pulled the third jelly jar wrapped in tinfoil out of her daypack. She cradled it briefly in her hands and then gave it to Dot.

"I have something to add," Dot said, taking the jar with one hand and holding the bag from her pocket with the other. "I didn't think I could say any of the right things, so I wrote them down and burned the paper. I want to scatter both of the ashes together."

Dot hadn't thought about the mechanics of doing this, so she stood still for a minute or so to work it out. Aunt Tab and Nick were quiet, giving her time to think.

Then she peeled back the tinfoil and twisted the jar lid open. A wave of dizziness swept over her, and she planted her feet more firmly in front of Dorothy Wordsworth's gravestone. She hoped she wasn't standing on Miss Wordsworth's head and realized she didn't know if people were buried with their stone at their head or their feet. Probably their head, she thought, moving back slightly.

She handed the jar lid to Aunt Tab and then opened the plastic bag and shook the paper ash into the jar. Some of it stuck to the insides of the bag, but she got most of it out. Then she extended her arm, as Aunt Tab had done over the Thames, and slowly rotated her wrist, tipping the jar upside down. The ash spilled gently in a zigzaggy pattern as Dot swept her

Thirty-One: Third and Last

arm a little to the left and a little to the right. The gray ash silently disappeared amongst the blades of grass and tiny daisies. Birds chirped and the river made whispery swishing sounds. Nobody said a word.

As she finished, she took a deep, gaspy breath, as if she were coming up from a deep dive and hadn't had any oxygen in a while. She dropped the jar and her knees wobbled. Aunt Tab reached out to catch her, saying, "Here, Dot, let's sit on the grass over there by the river. There's more room."

When they had arranged themselves by the river bank, Aunt Tab took out the gingerbread and passed it around. Dot still hadn't said anything.

Nick pulled a book out of his back pocket. "Dorothy Wordsworth kept a journal, you know." He opened the book and began reading:

Grasmere looked so beautiful that my heart almost melted away. It was quite calm only spotted with sparkles of light. The church visible. On our return all distant objects had faded away—all but the hills...presently we saw a raven very high above us—it called out and the Dome of the sky seemed to echo the sound—it called again and again as it flew onwards, and the mountains gave back the sound...a musical bell-like answering...

Nobody said anything. Dot chewed a little gingerbread. It wasn't bad, she thought, but drier than her mother's. She kept her eyes on the Wordsworths' graves.

After a while, Aunt Tab said, "Time to go, kiddos. Other people need to commune here, too."

Dot looked around and noticed that other visitors were in the cemetery, talking and taking pictures of the Wordsworths' graves. Children were running around eating gingerbread and picking the daisies. The sun was shining, and she heard church bells ringing from somewhere across the river. She stood up, knowing she belonged in this **AT** world.

Thirty-Two: Time to Decide

On the bus ride back, Aunt Tab was full of instructions about how they had to pack up and catch their train back to London later that afternoon. They would spend their last night in London and fly home to Seattle the next morning. Dot was still quiet, mostly looking out the bus window. Nick, across from them, was reading more of Dorothy Wordsworth's journal.

Dot was thinking about Junie. If stayed in England, or went to Italy with Nick, she knew she'd miss Junie. She was already missing her, and missing people was hard. It tired her out and made her grumpy, all this missing. But she could feel England getting under her skin, becoming a part of her. England had taught her a lot, and she could tell there was a lot left to learn.

Aunt Tab turned to Dot and said, "When we get home, the first thing we'll do is go grocery shopping. We can make a list on the plane."

Dot's tired grumpiness grew. She wanted to go home, but she didn't. She wanted to see Junie, but she also wanted to explore this wonderful Lake District. She'd crossed a street by herself; who knew where she could go next? Italy? But a tiny part of her wanted to go back to school. But not the library. Not yet. Maybe not ever.

The tarot cards had said she had to make up her own mind. Miss Wordsworth, Miss Wollstonecraft, and Miss Austen had told each other, and shown Dot, how they had made their choices and lived with the consequences, both good and difficult. As all this spun around in Dot's head, she thought it would take a double dose of Tinkerbell and *Dancing on the Edge* together to help her make her own right choice.

Thirty-Two: Time to Decide

She looked out the bus window at the green and lavender hills beyond the road, and imagined a huge *Dancing on the Edge* spread out, billowing and floating across the entire landscape. Her mother's embroidered words,

Be Loyal
Be Daring
Be Inventive

would write themselves magically across the sky and dissolve into pixie dust that would make all the people alive again. And no trucks. A perfect world for loyal, daring and inventive Dorothy Mary-Jane.

The bus rumbled down a cobblestone street into Keswick and stopped by the grocery store. When they were all back on the sidewalk, Nick didn't say good-bye but walked with them back to The Star of Alethea. "Are you sure your doctor said all this walking was okay?" Aunt Tab asked.

"Oh, yes, ma'am. I'm supposed to."

At the front door, Nick asked Dot to sit outside with him for a few minutes.

"Okay. I'll be right up, Aunt Tab," she said as she and Nick sat on a bench outside the pub's front door, facing a slivery view of the lake and Catbells on the other side.

"Thought we'd never get rid of her," Nick said.

"What? That sounds like the old Nick."

"Sorry. I can't become perfect overnight. But I *am* sorry." He looked moodily at his splinted ankle. "So, are you going to run away or not?"

"I don't know. I want to, but I don't. I want to stay here, but I don't want any more partings, any more separations. I'm surprised I care, but I don't even want Aunt Tab to feel bad. And my friend Junie…" Dot dwindled off.

"But what about your own life? Doesn't that count for something?"

"Well, yeah."

"So do it! You can stay in the flat where I'm at. Nobody's expecting me home for a few more days. We can figure out where we'll go next. I have a bank account. We'll be fine." There were spots of color on Nick's cheeks as his voice rose.

Dot thought about Mary Wollstonecraft daring to go to Paris during the French Revolution and how her daughter, Mary, had run away with the poet Shelley and written *Frankenstein*. She thought about Jane Austen and her novels and how she and Dorothy Wordsworth were so attached to their families. She thought about Aunt Tab and how she'd showed up in the Quiet Room at the hospital, angry and protective. Mostly, she thought about her mother, and how she was here and not here. With such a flock of estimable women advisors, the answer should have been clear, but life was more complicated than that and besides, the whole world seemed to be telling her to think for herself and make up her own mind.

"I still don't know, Nick, I need to figure it out myself. I'm going to go pack, and I'll either come to your place or I won't."

"I hope you come," Nick said, looking straight into her eyes. Feeling a little hypnotized, Dot returned his gaze. He took her hand and held it between both of his. She liked how his skin was warm against hers. "Thanks for rescuing me," he said, "and thanks for letting me come this morning."

Dot finally extricated her hand and got up from the bench, almost tripping over Nick's splinted ankle as she turned and walked into The Star of Alethea. In the lobby, she noticed there was an older woman behind the counter. She went over to ask her a question.

"What does 'Alethea' mean?" Dot asked.

"It's from the Greek, young lady, and it means truth. Sometimes it's spelled T-h-e-a."

"Oh," said Dot, and went upstairs, smiling.

• • •

Aunt Tab was almost finished packing. "There you are, Dot. Better get a move on."

Thirty-Two: Time to Decide

Dot unzipped her suitcase. This time she started with *Dancing on the Edge*, folding it carefully and laying it gently in the bottom. Then came all the rolled up clothes, clean and dirty mixed together. Then the books. Then Tinkerbell, right on top. But when she tried to close her suitcase, it wouldn't zip.

"Aunt Tab, can you zip this thing? Or take some of my stuff in your bag?"

But Aunt Tab's bag was full and even she couldn't close Dot's zipper. Dot stared at her bag and then walked to the window to look out at this landscape that had come to mean so much to her. She had always taken her beautiful Seattle landscape, the snowy mountains, the water, the trees for granted. Now she knew there were beautiful spots in other places, too, and that her mother wasn't just in one place or in one time. In her own mind, Dot was no longer just in one place or in one time, either.

She walked back over to her suitcase and took out Tinkerbell and her pad of paper.

"I'll be right back, Aunt Tab."

"Not more than fifteen minutes," replied her aunt.

Dot ran back down the stairs and out the lobby door. She didn't even look out for trucks as she hurried down the sidewalk toward Nick's, although she did stay to the inside, away from the curb, and crossed the street only when other people were crossing, too.

When she arrived at Nick's door, she looked up, hoping he wouldn't be at the window. She didn't want anything to change her mind. Good, he wasn't there. She sat down on his front stoop, laid Tinkerbell over her knees and wrote a quick note.

Hi Nick,

I can't stay. I have to go home. But this is one of my homes, too, and I'll be back. After all, my mom's here now. I'm leaving Tinkerbell for you. She means a lot to me, I hope I can see you both again someday. And say hi to your sister.

Your friend, the Travelling Fool,
Dorothy Mary-Jane

    She folded the letter and rolled Tinkerbell around it. Then she leaned Tink against the door and walked away.

--Finis--

More, if you are interested...

<u>Books about Dorothy Wordsworth, Mary Wollstonecraft and Jane Austen:</u>

Gittings, Robert and Jo Manton, *Dorothy Wordsworth*, New York: Oxford University Press, 1988. The only real biography of the elusive Dorothy Wordsworth, so often overshadowed by her brother.

Gordon, Lyndall, *Vindication: a Life of Mary Wollstonecraft*. New York: HarperCollins, 2005. A sensitive biography of the energetic and headstrong Mary Wollstonecraft. Makes you wish she had lived longer.

Weldon, Fay, *Letters to Alice on first reading Jane Austen*. New York: Carroll & Graf, 1990. First published in 1984. A wonderful introduction to what life was really like in the late 1700s and early 1800s, and why it is good and fun to read real literature. Written as letters from an aunt to a niece.

Winwar, Frances, *Farewell the Banner "...Three Persons and One Soul..." Coleridge, Wordsworth and Dorothy*. New York: Doubleday, 1938. This book is probably hard to find, but is a delightful telling of the tale of these three interdependent and memorable people.

<u>Books by Dorothy Wordsworth; Mary Wollstonecraft; her daughter, Mary Shelley; and Jane Austen:</u>

Austen, Jane, *Pride and Prejudice*. New York: Penguin Books, 1996. First published in 1813. Jane loved the two sensible and lovely eldest sisters she created for the Bennet family. Mrs. Bennet is a perfect

More, if you are interested...

        example of a useless mother. All of Miss Austen's women must cope with the fact that the job market was entirely closed to them—although most chose marriage as the only means to survival, Miss Austen herself did not.

Shelley, Mary, *Frankenstein*. Mary's mother, Mary Wollstonecraft, died giving birth to Mary Shelley. The story of Frankenstein and his Monster has been accurately described by Dot in the preceding pages. Available free online at www.gutenberg.org.

Wollstonecraft, Mary, *A Vindication of the Rights of Woman*. New York: Penguin, 2004. First published in 1791, it was the first book to come right out and say that women should have the same rights to education, property, and work as men. This was a shocking thing to say, and almost nobody agreed with her.

Wollstonecraft, Mary, *Maria, or the Wrongs of Woman*. Not quite finished before she died in childbirth, this is Mary's attempt to put her passionate thoughts about society's ill-treatment of women into a fictional setting. This gloomy story was edited and published by her grieving husband, William Godwin. Available free online at www.gutenberg.org.

Wordsworth, Dorothy, *The Grasmere Journals*. New York: Oxford University Press, 1991. Allows you to follow Dorothy in and out of the drafty Dove Cottage, help her in the garden, and accompany her on her moonlit walks in the Lake District.

Dot to Dot

Dorothy Mary-Jane's
ENGLAND

Keswick

Alton London

Ideas and Questions to Think About

1. Sometimes people don't like to bring up the fact that a person has died because they "don't want to remind" family members or friends of their grief. Do you think this makes sense? Do you think Dot or Aunt Tab ever forgot that Thea had died?
2. Aunt Tab says that travel teaches you as much about your home and about yourself as it does about the new place you are visiting. Does this seem true? If you have had that experience, what have you learned about yourself or where you are from?
3. Dot notices that England and America used to be enemies, but now they're not. The same thing happens with people, as Dot discovers with Nick. How could knowing that this pattern sometimes happens change the way you act toward people you don't like?
4. Have you ever thought of running away? Dot thought of a few of the problems (no money, missing school, missing Junie) she would encounter if she decided to run away. But there are lots of other difficulties—make a list of ten things a kid would need to consider before running away.
5. Historical characters like Dorothy Wordsworth, Mary Wollstonecraft and Jane Austen may not be walking around in the present, but they wrote down their thoughts for us in the future to read. When living people read and think about the ideas of a dead person, in what ways does that make them still alive?
6. Dot learns about making her own decisions in this story. It takes courage and clear thinking not to be swayed by what everyone else

Ideas and Questions to Think About

is doing or saying. Think of examples where you or someone you know or have read about has made important decisions that go against what everyone else says.

Note from the Author

They say it takes a village to help parents raise a child. It's the same with books. Authors need a lot of help. Nobody writes a book on their own, even if there's only one name on the cover. A whole world of people helped raise *Dot to Dot*.

Dot has been three entirely different people over about a million drafts, and the problems she's faced have been all over the map. At first Dot was a rambler in her thirties, spending time in England for no particular reason. She was fixated on Jane Austen, but nothing much happened. My agent, the gentleman scholar A.L. Hart liked it because it had a long riff in it about hating computers. But nobody else gave it a second look, so we shelved it and then I wrote *Miss Alcott's E-Mail*, which a lot of people, including publisher David Godine, did like. After the excitement of *Miss Alcott* died down, I pulled out Dot again and added an actual storyline. This time Dot was in her fifties and had marital and job complications that sent her to England, where she got the historical help she needed. But the plot was too complicated and I wasn't competent enough to control it.

Then my husband suggested I write the story from the point of view of a young person. Might be more fun, and maybe more useful too. So I did, and now it's in your hands. And head.

Thanks to the editors and critics of all three versions. Everyone helped. Here's just a few of the people who cared enough to tell me what they thought and to cheer me up when all seemed bleak and pointless: Joy Selak, Katherine Brown, Deborah Burand, Sandi Kurtz (who supplied the sugar cubes), Cindy Ayers, Marcia Cantarella, Nancy Kirk, Sue Berger

Note from the Author

Ramin, Heather Barbieri, Gennie Winkler, Barbara BonJour, Josie Kearns (who read the tarot cards) and everyone else at the wonderful Ragdale Artists' Residency, including Stephanie Kallos, who got me there, Reko and Samantha Sullivan, Grace Lynch, Emma Chrisman, Liz Allyn, Anjali Banerjee, Spring Zoog, and, especially and for always, my estimable Seattle-7Writer comrades.

Gracious hosts and helpers in England include Gail and Michael Thompson, the staff at the Wordsworth Trust, Jane Austen's House Museum, The Chawton House Library, and the extremely generous and knowledgeable Jeronime Palmer and her family at Greta Hall. The talented Ana Todd designed the cover, and the editors and designers at Amazon's CreateSpace deserve a thank-you cheer, too. Without them all, Dot would never have seen the light of day. Not forgetting, of course, my practically perfect husband Peter Russo and our entirely perfect daughters Tess Russo and Maya Noren—they are really the ones who make it all happen.

Kit Bakke
kit@kitbakke.com
www.kitbakke.com
www.seattle7writers.org
Seattle, 2011

Made in the USA
Charleston, SC
15 June 2011